"We'll leave tomorrow on the stage, unless ya need to rest a spell..."

She put one hand on her belly and the other on her chest, as if checking to make sure she was all there. "I am very tired. I hope that's not an inconvenience."

Oscar studied her again. She had a calm demeanor; he liked that, too. "Not at all. I'll take you to the hotel. We can eat and..." He glanced at Irene, still paying far too much attention to his affairs. "...figger out what we'll do after ya rest."

His future bride giggled—a good sign. "Get married, I would imagine." She looked away as she brushed at her skirt.

He smiled. She was scared, tired, hungry, but was doing her best to appear calm and collected. She was a real lady—he could tell by how she stood so straight, almost regally. But if that was so, why were her clothes so ragged? Something didn't add up.

Kit Morgan has written all her life. Her whimsical stories are fun, inspirational, sweet and clean, and depict a strong sense of family and community. Raised by a homicide detective, one would think she'd write suspense, but no. Kit likes fun and romantic Westerns! Kit resides in the beautiful Pacific Northwest in a little log cabin on Clear Creek, after which her fictional town that appears in many of her books is named.

His FRONTIER MOUNTAIN FIANCÉE

KIT MORGAN

Previously published as *Dear Mr. White*

ISBN-13: 978-1-335-14671-7

His Frontier Mountain Fiancée

First published as Dear Mr. White in 2017 by Kit Morgan. This edition published in 2020.

Copyright © 2017 by Kit Morgan

This edition published by arrangement with Harlequin Books S.A.

For questions and comments about the quality of this book, please contact us at CustomerService@Harlequin.com.

Harlequin Enterprises ULC
22 Adelaide St. West, 40th Floor
Toronto, Ontario M5H 4E3, Canada
www.Harlequin.com

Printed in U.S.A.

His
FRONTIER
MOUNTAIN FIANCÉE

Chapter One

The office of Mrs. Adelia Pettigrew (aka the Mad Matchmaker), 1901

Dear Mrs. Pettigrew,

My name is Oscar White. I run a stage stop with my family between Clear Creek and Oregon City, Oregon. We homesteaded here in 1849. I live with my two younger brothers, Henry and Anson, and our mother.

After careful consideration, I find myself in need of a wife. I'm not getting any younger and figured it was time. I am forty-five years of age, a simple man with simple needs. I am tall, so a woman of some height would be good. I work hard as does my family, so don't need no wilting flower. She's got to be strong and able to help my ma and me run things. That means cooking, sewing, mending, the usual chores for

*women folk. She's also got to be good-natured.
We run a fine stage stop and have a good reputation. I don't want it sullied by some woman
with bad manners and a temper.*

*Respectfully yours,
Oscar White*

Mrs. Pettigrew's assistant, Fantine Le Blanc, set
the framed letter on her boss's desk, then glanced
at the walls of the office. They were covered with
framed letters from mail-order brides Mrs. Pettigrew
had sent off to be married. Since she was hired, her
boss had taken the time to tell her the stories behind
some of the letters. "I do not understand, *Madame*.
What is so special about *this* letter?"

"Did you not say you wanted to hear a tale of a
different sort, *ma cherie*? Well, this tale is very different indeed."

"It is? And it takes place in Clear Creek, the same
town in the story you told me several months ago?"

"*Oui, ma petite.* But only part of this tale takes
place in Clear Creek. Most of it centers around *Monsieur* White and his family, who lived more than several days' ride away. Even now, with better roads and
good horses, one cannot make the trip in less than a
few days. Or so I am told."

Fantine's eyes grew wide. "The Whites lived an...
isolated life."

"Not so much—they ran a stage stop, after all.

How lonely could they be with people coming and going all the time?"

"Like a hotel of sorts?"

"Of sorts." Mrs. Pettigrew's face had a far-off look, as if she'd been to the stage stop herself. "It is a sad tale, yet a happy one."

"Sad? But why?"

Mrs. Pettigrew smiled. "Ah, *ma belle*, you are so young, so innocent. You did not live through it."

"Through what?"

For the first time Fantine could recall, her employer looked anguished. "The war, my child." The woman swallowed, as if she could not go on.

She had told Fantine other tales of people who'd been in The War Between the States, such as Pleasant Comfort, whose family lost their plantation because of the war. But that story hadn't made Mrs. Pettigrew look distraught. But… Pleasant had married one Eli Turner in 1877. She looked at the date on Oscar White's letter again. "March 31, 1875," she read aloud. "The war was ended some ten years when he wrote this."

"Oui, *cherie*, so it was. Not so long at all."

"And did not a man named White wed Eli Turner's younger sister?"

"Oui." Mrs. Pettigrew slowly nodded, still staring off into the distance. "She married Anson White, Oscar's younger brother, not more than a year before Eli married Pleasant Comfort." She took a deep breath and fingered the inkwell on her desk.

"*Madame* Pettigrew…why do you look so sad?"

"Because I am reminded of how cruel people can be when I think of Oscar and his bride. I was so much younger then, still so innocent in the ways of the world. So much cruelty during the war, *ma douce*, and then so much cruelty after." She shoved the ink-well aside, her face back to normal.

"What sort of cruelty, *Madame* Pettigrew?" Fantine asked tentatively.

Mrs. Pettigrew folded her hands on the table in front of her. "The worst sort. The kind fueled by jealousy, greed, contempt."

Fantine's brow knit in worry. "What happened?" she asked in a small voice.

Mrs. Pettigrew sighed, opened the top drawer of her desk, pulled out a lace handkerchief and offered it to Fantine. "Take it, *ma chere*. You will need it for this story."

Fantine's eyes went round as platters. "I do not think I wish to hear this story, *Madame*."

Mrs. Pettigrew smiled gently. "Ah, but you do, or you would not have asked. And though it is full of the cruelty of men, it is not only about that."

Fantine didn't look convinced, but she took the handkerchief. "What sort of woman did you send Mr. White?"

"One perfect for him."

Fantine's eyes flicked to the letter and back. "She was tall, strong and had nice manners?"

"Oh, no. She was not what *Monsieur* White

wanted. But she was exactly what he *needed*—and he was what she needed."

"Needed, *Madame*?"

"*Oui*. And her name, *ma petite*, was Lily Fair…"

Denver, Colorado, March 1875

Lily Fair Olson sat across the desk from Mrs. Pettigrew, the newest matchmaker in town. She couldn't be much older than Lily Fair herself, perhaps not older at all. What had drawn the widow into the matchmaking business? Lily had always looked down on such enterprises before—what kind of woman had to resort to answering advertisements from men looking for brides? Now she knew—desperate ones. Like herself.

"I am afraid I have only the one applicant, *ma cherie*," Mrs. Pettigrew told her in a French accent, or at least an attempt at one. Heaven only knew which.

"Is he…a nice man?" Lily asked, her eyes darting to the man's application on the desk. "A tolerant man?"

Mrs. Pettigrew sat across the huge desk and studied Lily like a wise old owl. With her bright blue eyes, dark lashes and eyebrows, charming face and raven-black hair, Adelia Pettigrew was a stunning woman. Not to mention a rich one, and a recent widow at that. Why would she take to matchmaking instead of marrying again? Undoubtedly she could have all the suitors she wanted.

Lily tried not to fidget. She was nothing like the elegant woman on the other side of the desk— probably older, with ordinary brown hair that only gained streaks of red and gold in summertime. Her eyes were brown and somewhat dull, though they hadn't always been. She was slim, nowhere near as shapely as Mrs. Pettigrew either.

She fought a sigh under the matchmaker's scrutiny. Why was she staring instead of answering her questions?

"I do not know," Mrs. Pettigrew finally said.

Lily closed her eyes and nodded. So she had no idea what sort of man this was, or what she was getting herself into. Still, it beat the alternative: abject poverty and utter destitution. "His name?"

Mrs. Pettigrew glanced at the paper. "Oscar White. He hails from Oregon."

"Where in Oregon?"

"I am sorry, but there is no town listed. Only that he is between someplace called Clear Creek and Oregon City."

"I have heard of Oregon City," Lily replied. Mostly she'd heard it was small, a speck compared to her native Charleston, South Carolina. That was a real city, even after the war's deprivations. But she'd been living with her aunt in Denver for years, and memories of Charleston were fading. And these days, her mind was so muddled from lack of food and sleep that she didn't care about them anyway. She just knew she had to survive.

She reached for Mr. White's letter and read it. "He runs a stage stop," she whispered to herself. Her eyes widened and a small smile formed on her lips. "This man and his family must live off by themselves."

"Quite right," Mrs. Pettigrew agreed. "It would mean isolation for you, in a way. Still, there would be no shortage of people."

"No, I imagine not," Lily muttered, her eyes still scanning the letter. She finally set it down and once again shut her eyes a moment.

"Are you quite all right, *mademoiselle*?"

She opened her eyes and stared at the matchmaker. No, she'd heard real Frenchmen in Charleston, and Acadians from New Orleans and Quebecois from Canada, and "Madame" Pettigrew didn't sound like any of them. That accent had to be fake. How odd. She shook off the notion and tried to concentrate, a hard thing to do when faint from hunger. "I will take him."

"Are you sure? You do not sound convinced."

Lily felt herself sway to the left and gripped her chair.

"Are you all right?" Without waiting for an answer Mrs. Pettigrew stood, went to the pitcher on a sideboard and poured Lily a glass of water.

She took it gratefully from her and drank. "I'm sorry, it is just that I have not eaten…in…"

Mrs. Pettigrew clapped her hands twice. The same young woman that saw Lily into the office— a maid of some sort, but without the usual uniform—

hurried in and curtsied. "Tea, quickly," the match-maker ordered, and the woman left.

"You do not want to wait for other prospects?" Mrs. Pettigrew asked and retook her seat.

"No, I can't. I must marry now."

Mrs. Pettigrew nodded in understanding. "He has sent stage and train fare. After you refresh yourself, you will write him a letter."

"Actually, I think it would be best if I simply went."

Mrs. Pettigrew assessed her a moment, but not cruelly. "No, *ma petite*. You must write him a letter so we may send it with your answer. He should at least know something about you before you arrive, *oui*?"

"But I don't have…that is to say…"

"And you will stay here until it is time for you to leave."

Lily stared at her in shock. "How did you know?"

"It was not hard to divine. Your dress is care-worn, patched in several places. You have dirt on your nose…"

Lily immediately rubbed at it in embarrassment.

"You have already said it has been some time since you ate. Conclusion: your money is gone and you have no home, or not an adequate one. You seek a husband to survive."

Lily stared at the woman in shock. She had said it so matter-of-factly, without the judgment most people carried along with it. "Yes. I do." She licked her lips, already dry despite just having had some water. "I'm desperate, you might say. And…"

Mrs. Pettigrew leaned forward, her big blue eyes full of compassion. "And what, *ma belle*?"

Lily met her gaze. "Broken."

Lily lay in the huge bed in one of Mrs. Pettigrew's guest rooms, staring at the crocheted canopy overhead. She'd had other lodgings, but had been forced to leave the drafty boardinghouse the morning of her interview due to lack of funds. At least she didn't have to live in the street her few remaining nights in Denver. Late March wasn't exactly the dead of winter, but with the "Mile High City's" position just east of all those snow-capped mountains, it was still too cold to sleep outside in a worn-out coat.

She fingered the frayed lace of her nightdress. She hadn't had new clothes for years. She'd led a life of privilege before the war—she and John had both come from prosperous plantation families. But the war took all of it, and then some. John was shot by a Union soldier at Chancellorsville, mere months after they'd wed. Her father, father-in-law, brother and two male cousins all died in the infamous Battle of the Crater in Virginia, and her mother was felled by a heart attack when she got the news. She, her mother-in-law and John's aunt were all that were left.

Then she lost John's mother to a fire when the soldiers came and ravaged South Carolina. What the Union soldiers didn't take or burn, the looters did, wiping them out. By then, there were no men to marry in Charleston save for the lame and infirm and a few Yankee carpetbaggers. Moving in with John's sickly aunt in Denver—she'd gone there due to tuberculosis shortly before First Manassas—was her only real option.

But what did it matter? she'd thought when she headed west to Colorado Territory. Her pain was too great. She couldn't marry again, not even to survive. Then Aunt Hortense coughed her last breath away, Lily at her side, without a penny to their names…and marriage became her only chance to survive, short of selling herself on the street. No money, no home, no food. Nothing.

And it was all her fault. She was Lily Fair Olson, daughter of generations of Carolina planters—too proud to work, too much a Southern Lady to get her hands dirty like common people. Oh, she did clean, cook and mend, as Hortense could afford no servants or slaves to do those tasks, but she'd made a hash of each task. And to work outside the safe confines of her aunt's home was unthinkable.

Looking back on it she should have handled things differently. She should have worked when she had the chance, done something, anything to take in money and tuck it away. At least now she'd have enough to start again someplace else. But no, she'd let her pride starve her instead, not to mention her aunt. She'd lived off Aunt Hortense's money, having none herself, until it was all gone. She'd held out for a miracle that never came.

Hortense had passed just as the money ran out. Her aunt always had been punctual.

She sighed and continued to stare at the intricate lace overhead. This time would be different. She was different—hunger did that to a person. And finding work in Denver wasn't a choice—what was she qualified to do save sit around, drink tea and waste money? If she didn't wed—and she had no prospects in Denver—the only other choice was becoming a "soiled dove," and at her age it was probably too soon to start even if she could stomach the prospect.

But then, would getting married to a complete stranger in the back of the beyond be any better? She'd still have to work—that was a fact of life that, before the war, she hadn't given a thought to. She hadn't considered it much afterward either, not until right before Aunt Hortense died and her precarious situation was staring her in the face. Now she had no skills unless you counted being scared out of her wits. She just hoped that by the time she got to Clear Creek, she found some of her old moxie.

Oh, she missed her old life. Her family and John's had fought for that old life, when not a day went by that she didn't have a myriad of slaves at her beck and call. Her father had owned dozens. But that life was gone, as were the now-freed slaves.

After, many a Union soldier blamed South Carolina for starting the war—they'd been the first state to secede, a founding member of the Confederacy, and the bombardment of Fort Sumter in Charleston Harbor was considered by many the first military engagement of the conflict. No wonder that near the war's end, when General Sherman marched his troops up through the Carolinas from Savannah…

Lily shuddered as a chill went up her spine. By the time Sherman and his armies were done, she was lucky to be alive.

She sent up a silent prayer for those left behind, families and friends she'd known whom now, years later, were in no better shape than she was. Perhaps she was doing the right thing after all. At any rate, it was the necessary thing—that would have to do.

Chapter Two

❧

Clear Creek, Oregon, April 1875

Oscar White wiped his sweaty hands on his trousers for at least the twelfth time before sticking a couple of fingers into his shirt collar to loosen it.

"If you don't stop fretting, Oscar, you're gonna worry yourself sick!" Irene Dunnigan looked at him with her signature beady-eyed glare, her face scrunched up. She'd told him that three times already that day, and at no point had it helped. "You know I'm right!"

"Yes, ma'am."

"Is that all you can say when a person's talking to you?" she barked back.

"No, ma'am."

Mrs. Dunnigan rolled her eyes and shook her head. "I'm gonna start on your supply list. You and that bride of yours gonna get hitched today?"

"Most likely."

"Jumpin' Jehoshaphat—you done said something besides yes or no!"

He glanced at her with a tight smile. "Told ya I could." Truth was, he was so nervous that not even the cantankerous Irene Dunnigan helped. He found it hard to concentrate on anything, like remembering what time the stage was coming in. He kept looking at his watch every few minutes...

"AAAGH!"

"Land sakes, man!" Mrs. Dunnigan shouted. "Get a hold of yourself! All I did was tap you on the arm!"

"Yes, ma'am," Oscar sighed as he turned to look at her. He was tall, well over six feet, and towered over her, though not as much as some of Clear Creek's more famous residents of years past.

He smiled at that thought. He looked forward to regaling his bride with stories about Clear Creek on the stage ride home. He hadn't brought the wagon, since he didn't need many supplies—what few things he'd bought he could bring back on the stage, rather than subject his bride to a long wagon ride at this time of year. Oregon was known for its unexpected spring downpours.

Irene's husband Wilfred stepped out from behind the curtain separating the front and back of the mercantile. "Howdy, Oscar," he said happily. "So today's the big day?"

Oscar nodded to him, then glanced over his shoulder at the front of the store.

Wilfred laughed. "Woo-ee, I don't think I've ever seen you this jumpy!"

"That makes two of us," Oscar said. He was a man of few words; he said what needed to be said and that was that. But how would a bride take to that? Sure, he'd been lonelier than a polecat these last few years—that's what prompted him to send for a bride in the first place. Not that he hadn't tried before. He had. Not long after the war, in fact. But that was long ago, and he'd abandoned the idea when he didn't get any takers. Maybe it wasn't meant to be.

But now that it was really happening, that his bride was almost there, he'd broken out in a sweat. Not only that, his hands were cold, and Heaven's sake, was he getting light-headed?

"Willie ought to be pulling into town any minute now," Wilfred commented as he looked at his pocket watch. "Then I'm guessing you'll be off to see Preacher Jo?"

Oscar nodded, fighting the urge to turn around and look out the mercantile's front windows again.

"Well, I must say, Oscar," Mrs. Dunnigan stated, without her usual rancor. "I'm glad you're getting married. I'm sure an extra woman around your place will be a big help to your ma."

"Ma thinks so too." He noticed Mrs. Dunnigan still stood next to him, three peppermint sticks in her hand. "Those for me?"

"Who else would they be for?" she snapped.

"Here, suck on one. Peppermint's supposed to calm the nerves."

"At least it calms Irene's," Wilfred added with a grin. "As much as anything does."

She narrowed her eyes at Wilfred before joining him back by the counter.

Then they heard the distinct sound of the stage as it rolled up in front of the mercantile and stopped. Oscar wiped his hands on his trousers again and began to crunch on his candy, sticking the other two in his trouser pocket.

"Here we go!" Wilfred said, rubbing his hands together in anticipation.

Oscar smiled weakly and faced the door. Everyone in Clear Creek knew Wilfred was a hopeless romantic and a bit of a gossip, and liked nothing better than to poke his nose into other folks' romances. But Oscar didn't mind. Besides, he'd need witnesses for his wedding—maybe he ought to ask Wilfred now if he'd oblige…

"Tarnation, will ya look at that?" Wilfred exclaimed. "Oscar, is that her?"

Oscar's thoughts of asking Wilfred *anything* vanished as he set eyes on the woman getting off the stage. She was younger than him, which he already knew—thirty-seven, and twelve years a war widow, according to her one letter. But her light brown hair had no gray, only a hint of russet. She wasn't as tall as he'd like. Hmmm…and not as hearty-looking as he'd hoped either. If anything, she seemed rather fragile...

"Well, ain't you gonna go out there and introduce yourself?" Wilfred asked.

Oscar swallowed hard, glanced at Wilfred and Irene, then took a deep breath.

Irene came over and gave him a shove toward the door. "Land sakes, Oscar, get it over with!"

Oscar didn't say a word. He'd needed Irene's push just to get his feet moving. He went to the door, opened it, mustered his courage and stepped outside.

"Howdy, Oscar!" Willie the stage driver called as he climbed on top of the stage to retrieve the mail-bag. "Brought sumpin' for ya!"

Oscar stared at the woman standing next to the stagecoach. She stared back, her eyes big and round like a fawn's. She did look delicate, and he hoped he hadn't made a mistake. He descended the mercantile porch steps to the street. "Hello," he said softly, not wanting to scare her. He knew he could look pretty frightening if he wasn't careful.

"Hello." Her voice didn't sound as weak as he'd expected, and she had a strong Southern accent—not country, but cultivated. "You must be Mr. White."

"And ya must be Lily Fair." He didn't tack on her last name. He knew she was a widow—the name Olson had probably belonged to her dead husband. He'd give her a new name today, washing the other away completely. "Lily Fair," he repeated, liking the way it sounded when he spoke it. "Yer real purty."

She blushed. "Thank you." She glanced at the stagecoach and back, holding up the satchel in her hand. "I have no other luggage. We can go now if you like."

Oscar nodded as he studied her. Thirty-seven... eight years younger than him, but she looked younger still. If he hadn't known better, he'd have pegged her at thirty. He reached for her satchel. "May I?"

"Oh, please." She handed it to him, her eyes flicking here and there before settling on something behind him.

Oscar turned to see Wilfred and Irene watching them from the mercantile porch, then turned back to his bride. "That's the Dunnigans—they own that place. We get supplies there when we come to town. Clear Creek's closer to us than Oregon City."

She nodded as she saw Wilfred's happy smile, glanced at the large colorful sign that read DUN-NIGAN'S on the front of the building, then took a shaky breath.

Now Oscar noticed the dark smudges under her eyes. "Ya tired?"

She nodded. "I must admit I am. It was a long journey—I'm glad I'm finally here."

He smiled. "Ya have a nice voice, if ya don't mind my sayin' so." A gasp sounded behind him, and he turned to see Irene counting on her fingers. She looked at him, flashed ten fingers, then two, and grinned. He rolled his eyes—*yeah, I just used a whole twelve words, try not to faint*—and turned back to his bride. "Would ya like somethin' to eat? Or head to the church first?"

"Church?" she said in alarm. "Oh, um… I suppose I could do with a bite."

"I got us a room at the hotel for tonight. We'll leave tomorrow on the stage, unless ya need to rest a spell…"

She put one hand on her belly and the other on her chest, as if checking to make sure she was all there. "I am very tired. I hope that's not an inconvenience."

Oscar studied her again. She had a calm demeanor; he liked that too. "Not at all. I'll take you to the hotel. We can eat and…" He glanced at Irene, still paying far too much attention to his affairs. "…figger out what we'll do after ya rest."

His future bride giggled—a good sign. "Get married, I would imagine." She looked away as she brushed at her skirt.

He smiled. She was scared, tired, hungry, but was doing her best to appear calm and collected. She was a real lady—he could tell by how she stood so straight, almost regally. But if that was so, why were her clothes so ragged? Something didn't add up.

"Where's the hotel?" she blurted, as if she'd caught him assessing her.

He pointed down the street. "Thisaway." He glanced again at the Dunnigans, and saw Wilfred waving, then taking Irene's arm. What in tarnation…oh, right. He was supposed to offer Lily Fair *his* arm. He did, and she took it without a blink. He nodded thanks to Wilfred and headed down the street.

Willie joined Irene and Wilfred on the mercantile porch and handed Wilfred the mail pouch. "That Oscar sure got hisself a purty bride."

"That he did," Wilfred agreed.

"Maybe so," said Irene, "but if he doesn't start saying more than three words to the woman, how happy is she gonna be?"

"Oh, I wouldn't worry 'bout that, Mrs. Dunnigan," Willie assured. "I've heard Oscar flap his gums plenty."

"You have? Oh, I suppose you have, as often as you stay at the Whites' stage stop."

"Yep. Oscar can talk well into the night if'n ya get him on a topic he likes. So can Anson, for that matter."

"What about Henry?" Wilfred asked, referring to the middle brother.

"He does his fair share, but ya gotta 'member he's kinda slow."

"Yeah, I remember," Wilfred remarked. "Haven't seen him or Anson in a while. Oscar's the only one coming to town for supplies lately."

"Y'all see 'em soon enough," Willie said. "I hear tell next time they come, Anson'll be comin' too. Their ma don't like to leave the place much, y'know."

"If they didn't live so far away, we could go see

them," Irene said. "But that's too far to travel for just a visit."

Wilfred sighed. "Sure is. Well, we'd best get gussied up."

"What for?" she snapped.

"They're gonna need two witnesses for the wedding. And what if Annie's busy and can't be one of them?"

"Wilfred, I don't recall Oscar asking you!"

"I'm volunteering and saving him the trouble. Now put on your Sunday best, woman."

"I can't—who'll mind the store?"

"I'll do it for ya," Willie offered.

"What? You?"

"Now Irene, it ain't like Willie hain't done it before. Besides, how long has Oscar waited to get hitched?"

Irene sighed. "Oh, all right. For Oscar."

Willie's eyes widened in surprise. Irene wasn't the type to just up and leave her store in anyone else's hands. Oscar must have a special spot in Irene Dunnigan's heart—maybe because they were both excellent cooks. To this day, she was still trying to pry his famous dinner roll recipe from him. Without much luck.

Lily did her best to remain calm. The man next to her was huge, intimidating, but his voice was gentle and reassuring. She hoped it stayed that way. She didn't want to be married to a harsh man, especially not one his size.

They reached the hotel in short order—Clear Creek wasn't big. But it had one of the nicest-looking hotels she'd ever seen. "My goodness."

"Yeah, Cyrus Van Cleet spared no expense when he built his hotel. Kinda fancy for the likes of Clear Creek, but he does all right."

She glanced up at him. "All right?"

Mr. White smiled. "When he first built it, there weren't no guests. Now he gets them, though—they stop off here on the way to Oregon City or Portland or even Seattle, spend the night and head out in the morning. Some like it so much they stay on a spell and catch a later stage."

"I see. Well, it looks very fine. How many rooms does it have?"

"Thirty-six."

"Quite a few for a town like this."

"I don't think he's ever had it full. We only got six rooms at the stage stop."

"Do they fill up often?"

He shrugged. "Depends on the stage and its passengers. Couples take one room, but if ya have six singles, then we're packed. Any more, passengers have to double up and share."

"Do you ever have more than one stagecoach stop for the night?"

"Oh yeah—two's average."

She nodded, calculating the work that would go

into housing, feeding and cleaning up after a dozen passengers coming through almost every day. Being Mrs. Oscar White would be a lot of work, but it beat starvation. Her only hope was that Oscar was a good man—she'd worry about the rest later. But as she was marrying him, she could only put off the inevitable so long.

Lily shoved the thought from her mind as Mr. White escorted her into the hotel. She relaxed a moment as she saw the inside. The hotel was indeed, beautiful. It seemed horribly out of place in the tiny town—you could drop it into the middle of Charleston or Columbia and it would fit right in.

A dark-haired man with smoked spectacles sat on a stool behind the front counter. At first glance it looked like he was reading, which he was, but… "Braille," she said under her breath. "He's reading Braille."

Oscar looked at her, smiled, but said nothing, just waited.

The man raised his head, cocked it to one side and sniffed the air. "Hullo, Oscar," he said with an Irish brogue.

Oscar laughed, making Lily jump. "Howdy, Lorcan!"

"And who is that with ye? Could this be yer bride?"

"Well, we ain't hitched yet."

"Still yer bride," the man pointed out, making Lily smile.

Mr. White frowned. "Ain't it supposed to be 'betrothed' before ya get married?"

"Oh, don't be so picky aboot it, Oscar. And isn't yer wedding day today?"

Mr. White scratched his head. "Might be. Is our room ready? My *betrothed* could use a hot bath and a rest."

"Aye, yer *bride's* room is ready. In fact, Sally's already heating the water." To Lily's surprise, Lorcan turned to face her as if he could see her. Uncanny! "Ye'll be wanting something to eat, and Sally needs time to heat a few more kettles. Would ye like to step into the dining room?"

She glanced between the men. "Y…yes, thank you."

Lorcan smiled, then turned to Mr. White, waiting.

Mr. White eyed him a moment, then suddenly straightened. "Sorry, Lorcan. May I present Lily Fair?"

Lorcan straightened and cocked his head again. "Lily Fair," he repeated in admiration. "Could ye come closer, lass?"

Chapter Three

Lily Fair gave Mr. White a sidelong glance as the Irishman hopped off his perch, came around the counter and leaned against it.

Mr. White unwrapped her arm from his, put his hand in the small of her back and gave her a gentle nudge. "This is Lorcan's way of tellin' who's who."

"What?" she said in confusion.

"Don't worry, he won't bite," Mr. White reassured as Lorcan held out his hands.

Lily exhaled and took them in hers, taking a moment to study him. He was tall, though not as tall as Mr. White, and conventionally handsome. Her eyes darted between the two, and a part of her wished Mr. White was just as good looking. He wasn't, but that was okay—looks weren't everything. And it wasn't as if her future husband was hideous—just average.

The thought left as Lorcan—what an odd name— abruptly sniffed the air, twice, three times. Behind the smoked glasses, his eyes were closed as if in concentration. When he opened them he was looking right at her. "Yer name suits ye, lass. I'm Lorcan Brody. Me wife Ada and I manage the hotel for Mr. Van Cleet."

She stared at him in shock. "You manage this place? By *yourself*?"

He smirked, as if he'd heard that question a hundred times before. "Nay, lass—I've my wife to aid me. And of course Sally, the hotel cook, and a few others we employ."

She leaned slightly to one side to peek at the Braille book on the counter. "I see."

"Ye smell like flowers. Where're ye from, lass?"

"Denver, most recently. But I was born and raised in Charleston, South Carolina." Recently she'd learned to add the state to the location. In the South, everyone assumed which "Charleston" you meant, but Yankees had that other Charleston in West Virginia...

"Ah, that would explain yer accent. Lily suits ye. Ye remind me of one."

"The...flower?"

"Aye. So now when I smell lilies on the air, I'll know it's ye."

She gaped at him a moment, then looked at Mr. White.

"Yer lucky," he said. "He says I smell like a tree."

She laughed, unable to help it, and smiled at Mr. Brody. "Everyone has a specific scent?"

"Aye. What I lack in sight, I gained in smell." He tapped his right ear with his finger. "And hearing."

Her smile was replaced with a look of awe. "That's amazing."

He shrugged and turned to Mr. White, something else she found amazing. One would swear he had his sight, the way he moved. "I'll get yer key."

Lily watched as he went behind the counter without laying a hand on it as a guide, and stood before a series of cubbyholes. Some had what looked like mail in then, while others had a key. Mr. Brody ran his hand along the bottom row, stopped midway, then moved his hand up three slots. He reached in, pulled out a key and turned to face them. "Here ye are, Oscar. Ye can eat first then take yer wee bride up to yer room. Let me know if by chance ye don't wed today, and we'll fix up a second room for ye."

"'Course," he agreed, taking the key and turning to Lily. "Let's eat."

She followed him across the hotel lobby, through a set of double doors and into a beautiful dining parlor. "Oh my."

"Purty, ain't it?"

"It most certainly is."

A plump woman, her blonde hair streaked with gray, emerged through a swinging door at the far end of the room. She turned to them, a wide smile on her face. "Oscar!" she called, holding her arms out wide. "Come here, big man!" She strode over and gave Mr. White a big hug.

Lily's betrothed blushed head to toe. "Howdy, Sally," he mumbled in return and gave her a perfunctory pat on the back.

She released him and looked at Lily, smile still in place and her blue eyes twinkling. "And you must be the bride! Oh, just look at you!" She looked a little closer and the smile dimmed slightly. "Well, nothing a hot meal and a bath can't fix. You've had a long, hard journey, I take it?"

Lily nodded. "Yes. Very." If the woman had expected her to dress better for the occasion, well, she would be sadly disappointed. Her traveling clothes were the best she owned.

"Come, sit, you two. I'll fetch you something to eat." She headed for a table, then stopped and turned back. "I'm Sally Upton, by the way. Oscar, where are your manners?"

"Sorry—this has been..." He glanced at Lily. "...a busy day already. Sally, this is Lily Fair."

Lily's eyebrows rose slightly. *He* thought it was a busy day? He wasn't the one that had just stepped off the stage and been run from pillar to post ever since. But then, he might be just as nervous as she was, especially if they were to wed within hours. *Don't judge, Lily,* she scolded silently.

But she was judging, despite her self-admonition. Her groom was big and clumsy-looking and, from what she'd observed so far, not very verbal. She had a fleeting thought that he probably couldn't read or write either, but quickly squashed it. He'd written the letter to Mrs. Pettigrew, after all—of course he was literate. Unless he'd had someone else write it for him…

"Pleased to meet you, Miss Fair. And, Oscar, you'll be glad to know I made your favorite pie today." Sally bounced off toward the kitchen. "Won't take me but a minute to get you both some lunch."

Lily watched her disappear. "Um…how often do you get to town?"

"Every few months or so. All depends on the need. Willie brings us supplies on his stage run often enough so we don't hafta. Bigger items, he can't— lumber, furniture, that sort of thing."

"No, I don't suppose he could," she said softly, staring at the well-appointed table as she sat. The china looked expensive, as did the silverware. Could it be real silver? All this finery made Lily feel small, dirty and woefully underdressed. Even Mr. White's rough linen shirt, wool trousers and jacket were in better shape than her attire. She fidgeted at the thought.

"Somethin' wrong?" he asked as he took his chair.

Her face slowly rose to his, not realizing she'd been so absorbed with the table settings. "Tired," was all she could manage. They studied each other for a moment, and she wasn't sure what to do next. She was nervous, admittedly—not only was she about to marry a stranger, but she'd be living in the wilderness from the sounds of it, visiting even the tiny burg of Clear Creek only a few times a year…

Lily! You're doing it again. Don't start complaining when you haven't even seen everything or met his family. Besides, you're not who you were—far from it. You're in no position to be putting on airs...

Sally reemerged, humming a merry tune, a small platter of fried chicken in her hands. She set it on the table and retreated to the kitchen.

"Sally makes great fried chicken," Mr. White commented. He twisted in his chair to look at the kitchen door. "I wonder if I should help her."

"Help her? But you don't work here."

"No, but I know what it's like to serve folks all day. We're in between lunch and teatime. Normally she's takin' a break 'bout now."

Sally popped in again, two bowls in her hands, and set them on the table with a happy sigh. "Now I think that's enough for a light lunch. Anything else?"

"Got any iced tea, Sally?" he asked.

"Certainly, Oscar. Be right back."

Lily watched the woman stroll toward the kitchen as if she hadn't care in the world. Maybe she didn't. Lily envied her.

As soon as Sally returned with their iced tea and left again, Mr. White bowed his head for the blessing. "Lord, thank Ya for this food, and for bringin' Lily to me safe and sound. I pray she gets what rest she needs before our weddin' and finds me to be a good and honorable husband. Amen."

She stared at him, her mouth half-open. He seemed humble—a good quality, especially for a man of his size. She wondered if he'd fought in the war, but decided not to ask. Instead she reached for the bowl of vegetables. "After we've eaten and I rest a bit, I think I'll be ready."

His hand, halfway toward the platter of chicken, stopped at her words. "Then I'd best speak to Preacher Jo while yer takin'… I mean…restin'."

Taking a bath? she thought to herself. *Well, it makes perfect sense—he can see I need one—but it was nice of him to not finish saying it.*

They ate in silence, save for Mr. White commenting on the food now and then. "Sally will have made my favorite pie recipe."

"Yes, she said that," Lily reminded him.

"I said it was my favorite pie *recipe*—it's easy to make, that's why Sally likes it. But she don't have the recipe for my favorite *pie*."

"And what pie would that be?" If she was going to cook for the man, she might as well know.

"My own *special* recipe. Don't worry, I'll teach ya."

She suddenly realized how much he'd been talking about the food—and *how* he'd been talking about it. Not like a customer, but like a fellow chef. "Mr. White…"

He reached over and placed a hand on hers, and she noted how rough his skin felt. Working hands, not like John's. "Please, call me Oscar. After all, we're gonna be married later."

She felt herself blush. "All right, Oscar. I just

wanted to ask—who does all the cooking at the stage stop?"

"I do most of it."

Lily hoped she didn't look too shocked. "Not your mother?"

"She does a little. But I'm the real cook in the family."

"You are?" This time she didn't try to hide her surprise. He didn't look the type to cook much, or at all, really.

"I got a knack for it—and I like to experiment. Ma's good, but she just makes the same things over and over. Runnin' the sort of place we do—well, ya want to be known for a few dishes, but…"

Her eyes went wide. "You sound like a chef."

"Chef? You mean a fancy cook?"

"Yes, that's exactly what I mean."

"Aw, I don't know 'bout that. I just like to cook, and folks 'round here say I'm good at it. I don't know if I could work in one of them fancy city restaurants. Sally could, maybe—in fact, I think she did way back when."

Lily studied the food on her plate, what was left of it—she'd eaten almost everything. Granted, as hungry as she was she would have regardless, but it really was delicious. "So if Sally is a chef, wouldn't you be one as well?" she asked, her smile a challenge.

Oscar thought a moment. "Well…she's a *really* good cook. And I think I am too, but…" He paused, then to her utter horror asked, "How 'bout you? Are ya a really good cook?"

* * *

Oscar cringed. Oh no—for Heaven's sake, what did he say? All of a sudden, his little bride looked ready to bolt from the room, run upstairs and hide under the bed. All he'd asked was…oh. Hm. Maybe she couldn't cook at all. That wasn't uncommon with mail-order brides—he'd heard stories, and knew that many women who took that route had little domestic experience. Darn it, he didn't want to embarrass her. "Well…what do ya like to cook?" he tried, hoping for a better response.

Lily Fair sat a moment before managing a lopsided smile. "I like to…um, I like to bake."

His face lit up. "Me too! I got me all sorts of rec-ipes I've come up with for new kinds of cakes and pies. I'll show them to ya when we get home."

Something flashed in her eyes at the word "home," and he cringed again. Should he ask? They were about to become husband and wife, perhaps that very afternoon. Didn't she know that meant she could tell him anything? But he was a stranger to her, just as she was to him. He couldn't expect her to trust him right off. "It's okay if ya can't cook. We'll just have some fun learnin'."

Her face relaxed into a tiny smile. "Really?"

"Sure. I enjoy teachin' folks how to cook."

Her mouth fell open. "I declare, I've never known a man that enjoyed cooking, let alone teaching it." She speared her last piece of carrot with her fork.

"Maybe you wouldn't mind giving me a few pointers on baking too?"

"Sure. It can be a time for you and me to get to know each other, right?"

She nodded slowly in agreement. "I'll try to be a good wife, Oscar. Really, I will." There was an odd hesitancy in her voice, as if she wasn't sure of herself.

"And I'll try to be a good husband," he said. "Otherwise we might drive each other plumb crazy."

The same tinkling laughter he'd heard before bubbled out of her now. He liked that sound and wanted her to do it again—he just wasn't sure how to make it happen. He didn't know her well yet, and it usually took him a while to warm up to someone. Well, he'd best warm up quick, considering he was going to marry her.

Sally brought them each a piece of apple pie and a cup of coffee and then retreated back to the kitchen. Oscar could tell Lily Fair was trying to figure out what it was about the recipe that Sally liked so well. "It's a secret."

"I beg your pardon?"

"The pie recipe," he said with a nod at her plate. "I gave it to Sally, but no one else."

She smiled at him. "Do you often keep your recipes so secret?"

He nodded, unable to hide his pride. "Why do ya think folks like to stop at our place?"

"Because the stagecoach does?" she said with a grin.

Oscar chuckled. "Not just the stagecoaches. Folks

come from all over just for supper. Sometimes breakfast and even lunch before they leave. We Whites
have a reputation."

Her smile grew. "Then teach me. Everything you
know."

Oscar smiled back. "Don't worry, I will." He
leaned toward her. "But yer gonna hafta marry me
first."

Her laughter again filled the air, and he smiled,
pleased with himself. He just hoped he was able to
please *her* enough to hear her laugh like that all the
time. There was an odd sadness about her that he
didn't think a hot bath would wash away.

The meal concluded, Oscar escorted her to the
front desk, checked with Lorcan about her bath, and
led her upstairs. He unlocked the door and handed
her the key. "I'm gonna go talk with Preacher Jo
while ya clean up. I'll be back in a couple hours to
check on ya. If you don't feel up to getting' hitched,
we can wait 'til tomorrow."

She smiled faintly. "You're very kind, Mr. White…
I mean, Oscar." She shook her head.

"Well, it'll be a long while before ya get a chance
to stay in a place like this again. Unless we hafta
come back to Clear Creek right away. On the way
home there's nothin' but a few ranchers that open
their homes to travelers—for a fee, of course."

"Of course. How else would they be able to afford
to feed a stream of travelers?"

He nodded, and noticed he didn't want to part

from her. "Guess I'd best be goin'." He handed her the satchel. "Did ya bring a weddin' dress?"

Her face flushed pink. "I don't have one. I was going to wear this." She frowned at her traveling dress.

"Ya look fine," he assured her. "Two hours."

She nodded. "Two hours."

Oscar left, striding down the hall to the grand staircase. He could feel her eyes on him as he made his descent, until she could see him no more. It was an odd sensation, one he'd never felt before, but he rather liked it. He was already feeling a strange tugging, as if something in her was pulling him closer. Maybe it was because she was so pretty. She had a good figure to boot. He hoped he didn't have to fend off lascivious travelers on his wife's behalf.

Speaking of that, he'd better *make* her his wife first. That thought in mind, he left the hotel in search of Preacher Jo.

Chapter Four

Lily scrubbed herself clean, washed her hair and tried to make her clothes look more presentable—mostly, pounding the dust out of them. She never realized a stagecoach could get so dirty until she'd ridden in one.

She dressed, put up her hair and, rather than wait for Oscar in the room, wandered downstairs to the lobby. She found the blind hotel clerk fascinating and wanted a chance to speak with him again.

But it wasn't the blind man that greeted her from behind the hotel counter when she descended the stairs, but a woman. "Oh, hello—you must be Oscar White's mail-order bride." She went to the bottom of the stairs and offered Lily a hand. "I'm Ada Brody. I help manage the hotel with my husband, Lorcan. You've met him, of course."

"Yes, earlier. Your husband is a remarkable man."

Ada smiled, glanced at the ceiling and sighed.

"That he is. He's upstairs playing with our daughter right now."

"A daughter? Do you have any other children?"

"No just little Aideen."

"Little? How old is she?"

"Barely three, but going on thirty," Ada said with a laugh.

Lily laughed too. It was nice to be able to talk with another woman. There had been a few female passengers here and there along the stage route, but she would never see any of them again. Which made her wonder... "This is such a lovely hotel—does the railroad plan to come here one day?"

"One day, I suppose. But who knows when? It's not like we're really on the way to anywhere except Portland and Oregon City—and neither one is what you'd call a big town."

Lily glanced around the beautiful lobby. "It does seem a shame more people can't see this place."

"Oh, don't think that we don't have guests. We have over half a dozen staying with us now, aside from you and Oscar. They're having tea in the dining room."

Lily couldn't resist the urge to peek past her to the room's wide entrance. Sure enough, she saw most of the tables were full of people enjoying tea. "Seems to me you have a lot of guests."

Ada gazed into the room as well. "Oh, that. Well, most of those folks are locals."

Lily blinked a few times—had she heard her right? "Locals? For teatime?"

Ada laughed. "I always love the surprise on people's faces when they find out. I guess Oscar hadn't told you yet—a lot of Clear Creek's settlers came from England."

Lily took a few steps toward the dining room, curious now. "You don't say."

"Would *you* like a cup of tea? I'll tell Oscar where you are when he comes in. Lorcan told me he went to speak with Preacher Jo and Annie."

That drew Lily's attention. "Annie? Preacher Jo?"

"Rev. Josiah King, but no one around here calls him that. And Annie is his wife—you'll like her."

Lily nodded, then studied Ada a moment. "You're not Irish, are you?"

"No, not at all. I came to Oregon as a mail-order bride myself, just like you. Lorcan and I were married in Oregon City."

"You were?" Lily said in surprise.

"Oh yes. Out of curiosity, where are you from?"

"Charleston, South Carolina, originally."

Ada's eyes lit up. "How lovely—I have an aunt and uncle there! My my, we will have to have a good long chat if there's time."

"Yes," Lily agreed, and glanced at the dining room once more. She wondered how she'd missed the voices that drifted into the hotel lobby—there were definitely some British accents in the mix. "I think I will have a cup of tea, if you don't mind?"

"Go ahead and take a seat anywhere. Mrs. Upton will see to you."

Lily nodded, unsure if she should indulge herself. After all, she had no money and didn't know how much this was going to cost Mr. Wh… *Oscar*. Speaking of which, he ought to be along anytime now. Maybe she should just wait in the lobby a little longer?

Ada noticed her hesitation. "Go on." She motioned toward the dining room. "Oscar isn't going to mind you having a cup of tea."

Lily blushed, nodded and headed for the dining room.

When she entered, the folks sitting nearest to the entrance smiled at her. Soon everyone took notice and nodded in welcome. She studied the dining room's patrons with interest—a mix of ranchers, farmers, a few obvious businessmen. Some of the women were well-dressed, while others wore simple homespun. Their ages ranged from schoolchildren to old and white-haired.

One of the latter, a well-dressed, wiry gentleman, got up from a far table and made his way to her, a smile on his face. "Well, bless my buttons, you must be Oscar White's mail-order bride," he said in a dry nasal tone that screamed *Boston*.

She stared at him, unsure for a moment what to say. Did everyone in town know who she was? "How do you do?"

"Very well, thank you," he said. "Allow me to in-

troduce myself—I'm Cyrus Van Cleet, your host."
He turned and waved to his table, where a petite
older woman sat with two other, younger couples.
"Please, come join us."

She nodded shyly and followed him to the table.
The two remaining men stood and she smiled to herself, immediately feeling more at home. Ah, gentlemen.

"Everyone," Mr. Van Cleet said as he motioned
to her. "May I introduce Oscar White's mail-order
bride." He suddenly turned to her. "My word, I didn't
get your name."

The older woman rolled her eyes, but with a smile.
"He gets more forgetful every day."

"That's all right. I'm Lily Fair Olson."

The two gentlemen bowed. "A pleasure to make
your acquaintance, Miss Olson," one of them said.
"I'm Harrison Cooke, and this is my wife Sadie."

"Pleased to meet you," Sadie replied, catching
Lily off-guard. Mr. Cooke's accent was British to
the bone, but his olive-skinned wife sounded like a
Southerner—no, a Southwesterner. Texas, maybe,
or even Mexico?

"And I'm Harrison's brother Colin," the other
gentleman added. "And this is my wife Belle," he
concluded with a wave at the woman on his right.

"Welcome to Clear Creek," Belle chimed in.

Another Bostonian—heavens, Clear Creek seemed
to draw people from all over! Tiny though it was, the
town was almost as cosmopolitan as Charleston. Lily

wondered if she'd turn around to see a Negro couple wander in next, or a French trapper, or some minor European aristocrat. "It's a pleasure to meet you all," she finally said.

Mr. Van Cleet pulled out a chair and motioned for her to sit. "Here you are, my dear." He glanced around the dining room. "Oh, Sally? Might we have some more tea, please?"

Sally Upton hurried to their table, smiled at Lily, snatched up the teapot and headed for the kitchen.

"Now," Mr. Van Cleet said. "Are you excited about your nuptials?"

"To tell you the truth, I'm mostly nervous," she said.

"That's understandable," said Sadie—or was it Belle? Oh heavens, she must be more nervous about her impeding wedding than she thought. She was already forgetting who was who. "You *are* about to get married."

"Yes indeed," Lily said with a smile. "Thank heavens everyone keeps telling me this is normal, or I'd be worried."

The table erupted in laughter. "You'd be nervous whether you were a mail-order bride or not," the other woman said. Belle, that was it—Belle from Boston, Sadie from the South. That would help her keep them straight. "I, for one, am glad I wasn't a mail-order bride. You're much braver than I."

Before Lily could respond, Mrs. Van Cleet chimed in. "Tell us, dear, where are you from?"

"Charleston, South Carolina. By way of Denver."

"What brought you to Denver?" one of the Englishmen asked—Harrison, she thought.

She put her hands in her lap and stared at the tabletop. "The war," she said simply.

Apparently it was enough. The couples glanced at each other and nodded sagely.

Sally returned with a fresh pot of tea and set it on the table. "Will there be anything else?"

"No, Sally, thank you," Mr. Van Cleet said.

Sally smiled and did a quick study of the rest of the patrons, then her eyes suddenly lit up and her smile broadened. "Well now, you're just in time!"

Everyone turned to see Oscar strolling over, grinning like the cat who'd stolen the cream. "Well, well, if it isn't Oscar!" Mr. Van Cleet said happily. "Come join us, son."

"'Fraid I cain't just now, Mr. Van Cleet."

"Whyever not?" one of the Englishmen asked.

Oscar's stiffened, but the grin remained. "On account me and Lily Fair here are gonna go get married."

Oscar watched his future bride turn white as a sheet. Maybe he should have waited until they were in private to say that. But darn it, he was as ready as he'd ever be and wanted to get this done. He was becoming more nervous by the minute and feared he'd do something foolish.

It was bad enough some folks, folks who didn't know him, thought he was dumb as an ox based solely on him being about the size of one. Even now, he recognized the glimmer of judgment in several men's eyes—strangers, guests of the hotel. Some looked like they'd be more at home down in Mulligan's Saloon, but he knew better than to judge on appearances.

Oscar focused on something more important to him than the opinions of strangers—his bride. "Unless of course you're too tired?" he tried as Sally poured her a cup of tea.

Lily Fair looked up at him. "I'm fine."

He sighed in relief. Maybe she wanted to get it over with too.

"Jolly good!" Colin Cooke said with a huge smile on his face. "You don't mind if we serve as witnesses, do you, Oscar? It's not every day we have a wedding in town, you know."

"Unless you wanted a private affair," Sadie Cooke quickly added. "We don't want to impose, but we would love to join you."

Oscar looked at everyone at the table, all of whom were looking hopefully back. *Oh, why not?* he thought. "If it's all right by Lily Fair, it's all right by me." She might want to keep their wedding small, after all.

She too glanced around the table. "I…I think it's fine."

Cyrus Van Cleet clapped his hands and rubbed them together in anticipation. "Wonderful! We'll go to the church, you two can get married, then we can celebrate with a wedding supper—my treat?"

Oscar laughed at the older man's enthusiasm. "Like I said before, it's all right by me if it's all right by her."

She gazed up at him and smiled. "Yes, I think I'd like that."

Good, he thought to himself. The poor thing didn't even have a wedding dress, but he could at least give her a few guests and a wedding banquet. And maybe she would make friends with the Cooke women and Mrs. Van Cleet and Annie King...who knew?

Cyrus jumped to his feet. "Wonderful! I'll go let Sally know what's afoot and we can be off." He hurried toward the kitchen.

"My," Lily Fair said, her hand on her chest. "I think he's more excited than we are."

"That's 'cause he's not as nervous as we are," Oscar pointed out.

The Cookes laughed as Harrison stood, came around the table and slapped Oscar on the back. "Congratulations," he said. "After the wedding, Colin and I would like to speak with you about something."

Oscar nodded, but didn't ask what it was about. At this point, he was so nervous that whatever Harrison said would likely go in one ear and out the other.

The rest of the party got up and prepared to leave just as Cyrus popped out of the kitchen. He went straight to Oscar. "All right, it's all arranged. Let's go have ourselves a wedding!"

The little group left the hotel, Oscar leading the way. He held Lily Fair's hand rather than escort her arm-in-arm. He liked the feel of her small hand in his, and thought the less formal gesture might relax her. Their guests trailed along behind, laughing and talking, lending the walk a festive air. He hoped Lily liked it.

Speaking of which... "Do ya mind if I call you Lily Fair? Or should I just call ya Lily?"

"I don't mind either way. Most folks simply say Lily." She looked up at him, but only for a moment.

Worry pricked him. "Everythin' all right?"

She swallowed hard and nodded.

He squeezed her hand lightly. "I'm jumpy as a junebug myself."

She turned to him in surprise. "You are?"

"'Course I am. Maybe more than you, seeing as I ain't never been married before. At least ya have some practice."

"Yes, I suppose." She sounded sad, and stared at the ground.

Oh darn, had he done it again?! He knew she was a widow and her husband had died in the war, but that was it. Maybe he hadn't been such a good husband, or he had and she still grieved for him. To Oscar, her past was just that, the past. He could leave it that way if she could. But maybe he'd better ask her about it sometime.

He was discovering there was a whole lot about marrying a woman that nobody'd told him. Every time he opened his mouth, it was like walking through a cow pasture—he really had to watch where he stepped.

When they reached the church, Oscar glanced over his shoulder and noticed they'd picked up a few extra wedding guests—Wilfred and Irene Dunnigan (he should've figured on them showing up), Patrick and Mary Mulligan who owned the saloon, and Doc and Grandma Waller, one of the town's founding families and oldest souls. He stopped to let them catch up.

"Thanks for waiting," Doc said happily when he reached Oscar. "Me and Grandma wouldn't miss this for the world."

"Land sakes, Oscar," Grandma Waller said, "why didn't you tell us you were getting married today?"

Oscar shrugged. "To tell ya the truth, Grandma, I didn't know 'til half an hour ago myself." He looked at Wilfred and Irene. "But being as how this is Clear Creek, news travels fast."

"I didn't say a word to anyone!" Wilfred said in his own defense. "Preacher Jo came into the store and asked Irene and me to be witnesses. You know as well as everyone else in town that I'm always a witness."

Oscar chuckled to himself and looked at Lily. "Wilfred never misses a weddin' if he can help it, so Preacher Jo finally made him the official witness for all ceremonies." He turned to Wilfred. "I did mean to ask ya earlier—I just forgot."

"Aw shucks, Oscar, you don't have to ask. You know I'd be there for you anyway."

"That's mighty nice of ya, Wilfred—thanks. You too, Irene."

Irene squinted up at him. "Don't mention it."

Oscar gave Lily's hand a reassuring squeeze as he led her into the church, their little company following along behind them. Patrick Mulligan had slipped into the sanctuary ahead of them and was speaking with Preacher Jo. He briefly wondered what they were talking about, then pushed it aside. He needed to concentrate on saying his vows correctly when the time came. He hoped he didn't get tongue-tied.

He tried to distract himself by admiring his future bride. "There's Preacher Jo," he finally said. "Real nice fella."

"Is the woman at the piano his wife?"

"Yep. That's Annie. You'll like her."

"I've liked everyone I've met here so far," she said softly.

"We don't get to town often, but when we do we have a good time." Oscar felt a pang of guilt that Lily Fair wouldn't see them again for quite a while, and then only if she came to town with him for supplies. That, of course, depended on how busy they were at the stage stop and if Ma could spare her.

She looked at him and smiled weakly, but said nothing.

He'd have to manage it somehow—he couldn't very well deprive his new wife of the company of women friends. True, plenty of women passengers came through the stage stop, but you couldn't make friends with someone who was there for only a night. Ma was willing to settle for just passing acquaintances, but that didn't mean his new wife would be. "What I mean is, go ahead and make friends today if ya can. We'll see them again. I promise. And ya can always write letters in the in-between times."

She smiled and nodded, looking over at Sadie and Belle. "I'd like that."

He let go of her hand and nodded in their direction. "Go ahead, talk with them. Looks like Mr. Mulligan's still speakin' with Preacher Jo anyhow."

She glanced at the front of the church where the two men stood talking. "Thank you. I would like to speak with them. It's just that I…I'm not sure what I'd say."

Oscar shrugged. "Whatever comes to mind, I guess. I know Sadie and Belle are both good cooks and belong to the ladies' sewing circle in town. Maybe ya can find out when the next meetin' is."

Her eyes met his, their soft brown sympathetic as if to say *thanks for trying.* "But what good would it do?"

"Well, Willie the stagecoach driver can deliver instructions from them. Ya can sew quilt squares or whatever they need and he'll bring them to town. That way ya can still be involved."

Her eyes brightened at the suggestion. "Hmmm. I hadn't thought of that before."

"Willie's kinda our connection to the world. How else do ya think we know what's going on in town?"

Her face broke into a warm smile. "Thank you, Oscar." She turned and went to join the other women.

Chapter Five

"Are you ready?" Annie King asked.

Lily stared at the minister's wife, a pretty woman with thick chestnut hair and green eyes. She was polite and cordial and the other women appeared to love her. But her neck was covered with old scars, and it was all Lily could do not to stare open-mouthed at them. She certainly wasn't going to ask her how she got them. "As ready as I can be," she replied, then looked at her careworn clothing and blushed with embarrassment. "I'm sorry I don't have a wedding dress."

"No need to apologize," Annie said. "Josiah and I happened to have the time to see you and Oscar wed tonight, and decided to take advantage of it."

"Still," Lily hedged, "I wish I had one."

"From what I know of Oscar," Sadie cut in, "I don't think he minds one bit."

Belle added a small giggle. "I have to agree with

Sadie. I think Oscar's too nervous to fret over it, so neither should you."

The women turned to look at her intended fidgeting next to Preacher Jo, his eyes darting all over. Lily knew he was giving her time to get acquainted with them before the vows. The saloonkeeper, Mr. Mulligan, was now busy speaking with Mr. Dunnigan, who owned the mercantile. They looked like they were telling each other jokes.

"Don't worry about a thing," Mrs. Dunnigan told her. "Oscar White's a good man, and his mother's a fine woman. You're marrying into a wonderful family."

Lily studied the cantankerous older woman, who obviously had a gentle side. "Thank you, Mrs. Dunnigan. That's nice to hear."

"Don't mention it," she snapped.

Lily hid a smile and glanced once more at Oscar. He caught her look and nodded. It was time.

Before she knew it, she stood before the preacher next to her future husband. The Cookes, Dunnigans, Van Cleets and their other impromptu guests sat in the pews behind them. Annie took her seat at the piano and played a hymn, and they all began to sing. Their happy voices brought tears to her eyes. They didn't have to be there, nor sing a pretty hymn for her wedding. But here they were, singing their hearts out and sounding like they were glad to be doing it.

Oscar reached over and touched Lily's hand. She shyly took his hand and was soon holding on to it for dear life. If she thought she was nervous before, that was nothing compared to how she felt now.

When Preacher Jo started speaking, it took her a minute or two to realize he was! She saw Oscar nodding now and then, and thought maybe she should do the same. Then his next words came as a shock: "I do." She felt her knees grow weak. Surely they couldn't be that far into their vows already!

But they were, and soon words were spilling out of her mouth right after the preacher spoke them. Then… "I…I do," she gasped.

"Then, by golly," Preacher Jo said with a smile, "by the power vested in me by Almighty God and the state of Oregon, I now pronounce you man and wife. Oscar, you may kiss your bride."

Oscar still held Lily's hand. He took the other and stared down at her. She noticed he wasn't breathing and started to worry. In fact, he was frozen in place, just standing there looking at her as if he couldn't believe what had just happened. Well, that made two of them. Wasn't he going to kiss her? She glanced at Annie, who smiled back, but it did nothing to calm her fears.

Preacher Jo cleared his throat. "Ahem… Oscar? Anything in particular you're waiting for?"

Oscar swallowed hard, his eyes still fixed on Lily. "Nossir, Preacher Jo. I just cain't believe I'm married to this beautiful woman in front of me. Maybe I *will* call ya Lily Fair, on account yer the fairest thing I ever saw."

Lily's cheeks grew hot, but her smile was genuine. "Does that mean you'll kiss me now?" she asked shyly.

Oscar grinned. "Sure does." He carefully pulled her to him as if she might break, lowered his face to hers, gently brushed her lips with his and took a shuddering breath. "Mrs. Lily Fair White," he said, trying the name out. "Lily White." He smiled again. "I ain't sure which I like better."

"Whatever one you want," she replied. "Or whatever fits the moment."

"I say," Colin said. "You mean like when Belle screams through the house 'Colin Bartholomew'? She always calls me that when she's angry."

His wife gave him a playful shove. "I do no such thing."

"Yes, you do, my sweet."

"I've heard you do that," Sadie added, nodding sympathetically.

Harrison laughed. "I'd say congratulations are in order." He stood, pulling his wife up beside him. "May we be the first to say how happy we are to have had the privilege to see you wed."

Oscar nodded at him. "Thanks, Harrison. Mighty kind of ya to say."

Colin joined them. "Perhaps we should have that little chat with Oscar now?" he suggested to his brother.

Harrison's eyebrows shot up. "Right—of course."

He turned to Lily. "But first I must kiss the bride. You don't mind, do you, Oscar?"

Oscar chuckled. "So long as Lily don't."

Lily blushed, not knowing what to do. She smiled at Harrison Cooke and shrugged.

Harrison laughed and gave her a quick peck on the cheek. "I know I speak for all of us when I say that we wish you both the very best."

Sadie smiled and took her by the hand. "Congratulations, Lily. Is it all right if I call you Lily?"

"Of course."

"I wish you could stay in town a few days, but I know Oscar has to be getting back to the stage stop. It's a lot of work for his mother and brothers to handle when he's gone."

"I understand," Lily said with a tinge of disappointment. "I hope I see you again someday."

"Why, of course you will," Annie said. "As soon as we know when the sewing circle is going to start another quilt, we'll send word with Willie. Don't worry, you'll get to be part of it even if you can't come to town as often."

"That's very kind of you. I have to admit, I'm excited to help with your next project. I...don't sew well, just so you know."

The women laughed. "Don't worry, neither did most of us when we first formed the circle," Sadie said.

"True enough," Belle added. "And we can write letters too. I know it won't be quite the same as seeing you in person, but…" She glanced at Sadie and back. "…at least it's a way to stay connected."

By this time Lily had tears in her eyes. "Thank you, all of you. You've been so very kind. I don't know what to say." Probably a good thing—she was getting choked up. Part of her felt like she didn't deserve their kindness. Ten years ago she'd looked down on women like these. Embarrassed, she looked at Oscar, who was immersed in conversation with Belle's and Sadie's husbands. No matter—she felt too overwhelmed at the moment to say anything coherent to him. If she opened her mouth, she was sure to babble.

She made it through the rest of the well-wishes, congratulations and promises of letters—even from Mrs. Dunnigan. When Oscar finally concluded whatever business he had with the Cooke brothers and rejoined her, she looked at him and smiled.

He smiled back. "Well, Mrs. White, are you ready for supper?"

She nodded, unable to speak. The other women seemed to understand, nodded, then took their husbands' arms and headed out of the church.

"Everythin' all right?" Oscar asked.

Lily nodded, still silent.

"C'mon, Mrs. White," he said gently, sensing her distress. "Let's go back to the hotel and have somethin' to eat to celebrate."

Lily forced herself to meet his gaze, and to speak. "Whatever you say, Mr. White."

* * *

Oscar leaned over to whisper in Lily's ear. "Harrison and Colin done gave us some cattle. Wasn't that nice?"

Lily shook herself and looked at him. She'd been woolgathering again about living so far away from town. "I beg your pardon?"

"Cattle. They're giving us some cattle as a wedding present. That's mighty nice of them, Lily."

"Oh…yes," she said in surprise. "How many?"

He leaned toward her again. "Two bulls and half a dozen cows."

She blinked. "Isn't that a lot?"

"Well, when Harrison married Sadie his new father-in-law gave him a thousand head. But for our family, eight is enough."

"A thousand head," she said in surprise.

"Well, Sadie's pa is a wealthy cattle baron down near El Paso. He wanted Harrison to join the family business, so he built up their ranch and gave them a thousand head to get started."

Lily could only stare. The Cookes didn't dress like they were rich, certainly not like she would expect rich cattle ranchers and their wives to. Then again, what *did* such people wear? How would she know—she was from the South, not the West. Perhaps here that was as good as it got—which would mean she didn't have to worry about her own tattered wardrobe so much. "That was very kind of them."

"Sure was. Ma's gonna bust a gut when she finds

out. Harrison said he'd have his foreman Logan bring them in a few weeks. You'll like Logan—he's a nice man."

"Yes, you mentioned him before, I think."

"I did? Gosh, honey, at this point I cain't remember much of the last few hours. I've still got my head in the clouds."

She studied him a moment, wondering at the endearment. That was the first time he'd called her "honey." She smiled as Sally Upton pushed a cart of food into their midst. The small wedding party took up two tables and were the only ones in the dining parlor save for two men in the far corner, who had the busy look of traveling salesmen—hotel guests, she presumed. She wondered what business they had in Clear Creek.

"Chicken and dumplins," Oscar said. "One of my favorites. I do like Sally's recipe." He glanced around, then whispered, "But I like my Ma's better."

Lily giggled. "Almost every man thinks his mother is the best cook in the world."

"Can I help it if mine *almost* is?"

"Almost? Why is she almost?"

Oscar laughed. "'Cause she says I'm better."

Lily found herself laughing with him. It felt good to be in better spirits, and to have food in front of her. Sally had set them up with a huge beef roast, savory vegetables, mashed potatoes and a few things she didn't recognize, in addition to the aforementioned chicken and dumplings. Her stomach rumbled like a steamship pulling into the harbor.

Oscar picked up the dish of chicken and dumplings and began to spoon some onto her plate. She sniffed at it. "Mm, it smells delicious," she groaned.

"That's because it is." Sally set the last dish—spoon bread—on the table. "Congratulations, you two, and eat up!" She spun on her heel and headed back to the kitchen.

Lily laughed again. "Is she always that exuberant?"

"Always," several at the table said at once, exchanged looks and burst into laughter themselves. Harrison calmed down first and said a quick blessing over the food before everyone dug in.

Lily was determined to enjoy this sliver of peace and calm and…dare she say, joy?…before she had to face her next fearful hurdle. Her wedding night. Frankly, she didn't want to think about that yet. Maybe if she were lucky, Oscar would stuff himself so full of food he'd pass out before they got to that. He was such a big powerful man, but seemed kind, gentle and concerned for her. Could she ask for anything more? Dare she? In truth she didn't think she deserved someone like him.

After tonight, he might think the same thing.

"Oscar, Harrison just informed me he's sending Logan your way in a few weeks," Sadie said.

"That's right," Oscar said. "To deliver our weddin' present. I cain't tell ya how happy yer husband made me, or how happy he's gonna make my family. Thank ya."

Sadie waved a hand at him. "Think nothing of it—we're glad to do it. I was just thinking…if Belle and I can get away, we might take the stage out to your place and visit with Lily and your mama for a day or two. Then Logan can bring us back."

"What?!" Harrison sputtered over his potatoes. "What's that you say, wife?"

"I think that's a wonderful idea," Belle said.

"Wait, wait," Colin objected. "Shouldn't we men have a say in this?"

Cyrus and Polly Van Cleet laughed. "Oh, let the women go visit, Colin," Cyrus said. "Besides, Mrs. White could do with a nice visit from Sadie and Belle, isn't that right, Oscar?"

"I wouldn't object," Lily replied.

"But if the stage stop is busy, there might not be much time for visitin'," Oscar said matter-of-factly. "More likely Ma will put the two of ya to work."

Colin broke into laughter. "Oh, then you *must* go visit, darling," he told Belle. "Scrubbing floors and changing bedsheets never hurt anyone."

"Careful, husband," she riposted. "You'll be doing that if we're gone for a while." She turned to Lily. "And with five children, that's a lot of bedsheets."

"Five?" Lily said in surprise. "My goodness."

"Don't worry, Mrs. Cooke," Oscar said. "We got six bedrooms, most with two beds in them. There'll be plenty of sheets to go 'round."

Belle glared at Oscar, while Colin laughed in response. The good-natured Cookes were a delight to be around—Lily wanted them to visit, even if they did end up working for Oscar's mother. "I'll try to make sure the work gets done so you won't have to do any," she assured them, sounding more confident than she felt. Well, she'd only said she would *try*…

"We don't mind pitching in," Sadie said.

I may need all the help I can get, Lily thought. She'd have to get used to hard work, even if Belle and Sadie came to lighten her load for a few days. Besides, if she kept busy enough, maybe Oscar wouldn't be put off by…

"Spinach?" Oscar offered, a bowl in one hand, a serving spoon in the other.

She sighed and nodded. Best not to think about it. In fact, if she had her way, Oscar would never find out. *But there's no getting around it. We're married now. He's going to find out sooner or later.* She just hoped it was later. She glanced at the next table, where Preacher Jo and Annie, the Dunnigans and the Mulligans sat chatting, eating and enjoying themselves. Once again she found herself staring at Annie's scars.

Lily glanced at Oscar, closed her eyes for moment and sent up a silent prayer: *Please don't let him be disappointed. Please don't let him send me back.*

Chapter Six

"That was some supper, wasn't it?" Oscar asked Lily Fair as they reached the door of their room. When she didn't say anything, he looked at her. "Somethin' wrong?"

She shook her head and smiled nervously.

He unlocked the door and pushed it open. "I guess this here's the part where I pick ya up and carry ya 'cross the threshold." He stood looking at her, waiting for her response.

She swallowed hard as her eyes grew round. Good grief, she wasn't going to bolt down the hall, was she? "I guess so," she squeaked.

"I don't hafta if ya don't want me to," he said gently. "But I think the notion's kinda romantic. Personally I'd like to carry ya across."

Lily's eyes grew larger. "You would?"

"'Course I would. Yer my bride and…well, I only plan on doin' this once."

She looked away. "So did I. Things didn't work out that way for me, though. I hope they do for you... I mean, for us."

Oscar picked up something in her voice—regret? He hoped it wasn't about him—he'd hate to think she regretted marrying him already. Land sakes, it had only been a few hours! He faced her, palms up in invitation. "May I?"

She studied him a moment, then nodded.

Oscar smiled in relief, bent down and scooped her into his arms. "Mrs. White, I'll never forget this moment. I hope ya won't either." He stepped across the threshold and into the room, but didn't set her down. Instead he studied her face, her hair, her eyes. She had beautiful eyes with thick dark lashes. He was still working to grasp that she was his. He'd seen beautiful women before—the stage stop was no stranger to them, given how many folks came through. But this lady, his Lily Fair, was his and his alone—

"Oscar?"

He shook himself out of his thoughts. "Gosh, guess I was woolgathering. I reckon ya want me to put ya down, huh?"

She smiled and nodded. "That would be good for starters."

"For starters?" he repeated. "Then what?"

She shrugged. "It's getting rather late. I think bed is in order."

He swallowed hard as a nervous tingle went up his spine. Oh heavens—bed. *With her.* His wife.

"Oscar?"

"Land sakes, there I go again."

She giggled. "Why don't you put me down now?"

"Um, sure." He set her on her feet and took a step back, as if she would break if he stood too close. "Can I get ya anythin'? Some water, maybe?"

She shook her head and covered a smile.

"What's so funny?"

"You are." She clasped her hands in front of her. "I have to admit I was nervous before, but…you seem to be more nervous than I am."

He stared at her a moment, then threw his head back and laughed. "Tarnation, woman, if ya ain't perceptive."

"So I'm right?" she teased.

Oscar stifled his chuckling, went to a nearby chair and sat. "All right, I admit it, I'm plumb nervous. I ain't never been this nervous in my life. I don't know how you brides do it."

She sat in the chair next to his, folded her hands in her lap and stared at them. "Usually the bride is more nervous than the groom."

"Why's that? If I'm this nervous, then ya must be going plumb crazy."

She chuckled. "Most brides are terrified because they're coming into a marriage with, um…no experience."

Oscar jerked as if slapped. "Oh yeah. That. But…

then ya shouldn't be nervous. Ya done been married before."

She nodded in agreement. "True…"

Oscar pulled at his collar. "So at least ya gotta few miles under yer saddle…" As soon as the words were out he grimaced, squeezed his eyes shut and had to force them back open. "I'm sorry, Lily Fair. That was a horrible thing to say. When I get nervous like this I can't talk right. Can you forgive me?"

She pressed her lips together and nodded, as if she didn't trust what might come out of her own mouth.

"What I mean is, when a person like yerself's been married before, certain things won't be as new as they might be…uh…" He gulped and glanced around the room. "…well, to me."

That got her attention. Her eyebrows slowly rose as comprehension dawned. "Oh. Oh dear. I think I understand."

"Really? I mean, do ya really understand?"

She quickly began to fiddle with the worn sleeve of her dress. "Are you saying that you've never… er…been with a woman?"

Oscar looked her in the eye. "Yes, ma'am, that's what I'm sayin'."

A shudder ran through his new wife—he wasn't sure how to interpret that. But her next words were clear. "Then might I suggest we take a little time to get to know each other?"

He sighed in relief. "Ya know what, Lily Fair? I like that idea just fine."

* * *

Lily Fair thanked the Almighty over the next several hours as she and Oscar took the time to get to know each other. That her new husband admitted he had no experience with women actually endeared him to her. He really *was* more nervous than she, and for good reason.

He'd probably worried she might think less of him for it, which of course was patently absurd. But then again, he was forty-five years of age—for a man to hold on to his purity for that long was unusual. Men were men, after all. Still, he'd spent most of his life somewhat isolated with his family, away from the rest of the world. Because of that, she could believe it.

"Henry's special," Oscar was saying, drawing her back into their conversation.

"How so?"

"On account he sees things different from you or me. Most other folks just call him stupid, but he ain't—he's just kinda slow. And he says things 'zactly as he sees them. There's an innocence in that, ya know?"

"Yes," she said with a nod. "I think I understand. Can he read and write?"

"Oh sure—it's just that he's not as grown-up as the rest of us. And it's not like he's thirty years behind, either. Twenty, maybe…"

She took a deep breath and let it out slowly, her brow creased in thought. "I knew someone like that once—Violet Margrave. She was the daughter of a plantation owner. Her parents kept her at home when the family was invited to parties and other social gatherings. They hosted events at their plantation too, of course, but one rarely saw her. I was never sure if she stayed in her room by choice, or her parents kept her there when company was in the house."

"That's wrong," Oscar said, his voice deeper. "Just wrong."

"I agree. But there are those who don't know how to properly handle someone who is…" She waved a hand in the air, looking for the right word. "…*different* from them. But I'm sure you don't treat Henry any different than you treat your younger brother Anson, do you?"

"'Course not. I look after both my brothers. And any man who'd harm either one of them…he'll be sorry."

She noted the flash of anger in his eyes and wondered what happened in the past to give him such a look. Should she ask?

She didn't have to. "Once some men came through, outlaws, and tried to steal our horses by tellin' Henry they bought them from Ma. Henry may be slow, but he ain't *that* slow. He chased one of them out of the barn with a pitchfork. Lucky for Henry the man wasn't wearin' a gun at the time—I guess he thought he needn't bother." Oscar chuckled at the recollection. "Then Anson came along, grabbed another pitchfork, and did more than just chase one."

"Oh my goodness, what happened?" she asked, a hand on her heart.

"He stabbed that fella right in the seat, and a few other places. I'm sure that scoundrel wasn't able to ride a horse for a month."

"But if they were outlaws, what did they do? Did they leave, or cause you trouble?"

"Oh, they tried to cause trouble, all right. And the rest of them *were* wearing their guns. I had to knock a couple of their heads together, and Anson clobbered another with one of Ma's favorite chairs. She was purty sore at Anson for that."

Lily covered her mouth to stifle a giggle. "Oh dear!"

Oscar nodded as his face took on a far-off look. "Then Henry took this bullwhip one of the stagecoach drivers gave him the year before. He cracked that thing and split one of them outlaws' faces wide open, starting right here." He pointed to a spot over his right eye. "All the way down to here," he added as his finger traveled to the right corner of his mouth.

At this point Lily's own mouth hung open, her eyes popped wide. "What did the outlaws do?"

Oscar rolled his eyes. "The darn fool Henry whipped tried to shoot him. But he had his right hand over his wounded eye, tryin' to unholster his gun on his left hip with his left hand. He got himself all kinds of tangled up and fell right over, his gun went off and he shot one of his partners in the leg. That fella tried to pull *his* gun while he was stumblin' 'round, wound up shootin' another one of their gang. Well, I figgered I'd better put a stop to it before they all killed each other…"

Ladylike or not, Lily burst out laughing. "Oh my goodness, that's terrible! Not that you put a stop to it, but that they kept shooting each other on pure accident."

Oscar smiled and nodded. "Yep. And all 'cause Henry wasn't 'bout to listen to no hogwash."

"I can't wait to meet your brothers and your mother."

"I cain't wait for them to meet you neither. I gotta say, I'm excited—Ma's gonna bust a gut when she sees ya."

"Because you're finally married?"

"No," he said. "She knew I'd get hitched eventually. It's 'cause yer so beautiful."

Lily quickly sobered. She unconsciously reached a hand up to her cheek and let it drift down her neck to her waist. "The Good Book says beauty is fleeting."

"It does say that. But that don't mean I cain't enjoy it while it's here."

She smiled. Oscar White was a big man, powerfully built, used to hard work. True, he wasn't much to look at—his hair was thick, dark and unruly, with streaks of silver. His eyebrows were also dark and thick and…well, joined, giving him the appearance of having only one. His voice was deep and probably scary when he was angry. In short, he could be a force to be reckoned with.

But he was gentle and deferential, and acted like a gentleman. He spoke well, albeit in a country drawl that betrayed a lack of formal education. (Not a surprise; where he grew up, they didn't even have a one-room schoolhouse, let alone tutors like she'd enjoyed.) He was obviously intelligent, and certainly not lazy. She liked him. She just hoped that after the next few days, he liked her as much.

"What're ya thinkin' 'bout, Lily Fair?" he asked softly.

She yawned in response. "Oh, pardon me. My goodness, it must be late."

"That it is. We're leavin' tomorrow. Maybe we oughta go to the mercantile first thing in the mornin' and see if ya need anythin'. Might be a long time before we get back to town."

She looked at him as a chill went up her spine. Would he want to exercise his husbandly rights now, or leave her be? "We should get ready for bed."

"Yep. I reckon so." He met her gaze and smiled. "There'll be plenty of time to talk on the way home. That suit ya, Lily Fair?"

She let out her breath, not realizing she been holding it. He was telling her he'd give her—and himself—more time. "Yes, Oscar, I'd like that just fine."

The next morning the newly married couple got up, dressed and prepared for the long journey home. Lily Fair washed her face, put up her hair and followed Oscar downstairs for breakfast.

Mrs. Upton was just as chatty as the day before, and presented them with a basket of food for the trip. "I hope it's enough."

"I'm sure it will be, Mrs. Upton," Lily said. And she was—the cook had to use both hands to keep it aloft.

"Oh, honey, call me Sally. There's no need to be formal."

"All right, Sally." Lily took the basket, and managed to keep it from pulling her to the floor. "Thank you so much."

Sally glanced at Oscar and Mr. Van Cleet, who stood talking on the other side of the dining room. "I never thought I'd see the day when a woman landed Oscar White. You're very lucky."

Lily smiled. People kept telling her that, and she was beginning to understand why. "Thank you."

Sally sighed. "There was a time I fancied Oscar myself. But it never would've worked. We'd have fought like nobody's business."

Lily was shocked. "Fought? But why?"

"Two cooks like Oscar and me in the same kitchen? Oh no, no, no."

Lily laughed, instinctively knowing what the woman meant. "Too much competition."

"You said it. Every cook has their own ideas about things. Now best you run along. The stage will be here soon, and I heard Oscar mention he wanted to take you down to Dunnigan's for a few things."

Lily nodded and strolled over to her new husband. Oscar turned to her as she approached. "Ready?"

She nodded and held up the basket, with an effort. "It's from Sally."

Oscar took one look at it and smiled. "Looks heavy—here, let me take that." He took the basket and lifted it up and down a few times. "Yep, Sally packed this, all right. There's probably enough food in here for an army."

Mr. Van Cleet laughed. "That's our Sally. Now the two of you have a good trip home and give your ma our best. We'll see you next time we go to Oregon City."

"Do you go to Oregon City often?" Lily asked.

"Not as often as we used to—we're getting up in years, you know. But we try to make it once a year. Best of luck to you both." He gave them a parting smile, turned and headed for the hotel's front counter. Lily watched him go with the sinking feeling that all the vestiges of civilization were going with him.

Oscar straightened and offered her his arm. "Well, Mrs. White, shall we?"

Lily smiled and pushed the dark thoughts aside. This was the first time she'd seen Oscar with that look on his face, as if offering his arm was one of the proudest moments of his life. Perhaps it was. She slid her arm through his and let him escort her out of the hotel.

When they reached Dunnigan's Mercantile, the stage was already parked in front. Seeing it made her realize how much she was looking forward to the trip. Oscar handed their basket to Willie, who put it inside the coach and gave them a big smile, showing his missing front teeth. "We'll head out in 'bout fifteen minutes, folks," he said, then went to tend the horses, while Oscar hurried them inside.

Now that Lily saw the mercantile's interior, she wished she'd come in earlier. There were ready-made clothes, bolts of fabric, tools, books, hair ribbons, cooking utensils, pots and pans, boots, shoes and all sorts of other goods that she hadn't seen since leaving Denver. Even though Dunnigan's couldn't match the inventory of the bigger general stores she was used to, it had a good variety. And it was the only decent mercantile for miles around, or so she was told. "Do you travel to Oregon City at all?"

Oscar shook his head. "Not unless we have to. Clear Creek is closer for supplies."

She frowned. That answered that question—Clear Creek was as good as it would get as far as civilization. But the people were nice, at least those she'd met so far. Then a thought occurred that hadn't before. "Oscar?"

"Yeah?"

She absently fingered a pretty green ribbon. "What happens if one of you gets hurt? There's not a doctor around, is there?"

"No, we mostly do our own doctorin'. Pa was a doctor."

She stopped fiddling with the ribbon and looked at him. "He was?"

"Sure. And he and Ma taught me and my brothers." He put a large hand on her shoulder and gave it a gentle squeeze. "That and faith in the good Lord has served us fine all these years, Lily Fair. Don't worry, we'll take good care of ya."

Lily's heart warmed at his words, and she smiled and turned back to the ribbon. She'd survive this yet.

Chapter Seven

Lily perked up as the stage turned off the main track onto a smaller path. "How far?"

"'Bout a mile is all," Oscar said.

She stared out the window and saw the forest around them. "It's beautiful here."

"We think so too. I expect Ma'll be standin' on the porch waitin' for us. Willie's pretty prompt."

She smiled. They'd spent the last few days talking and getting to know each other. He'd told her how his family had stopped in the area years ago when they were part of a wagon train heading west. His mother was expecting Anson any day, and the family stayed behind on the Oregon Trail so she could deliver as the other wagons moved on. Anson was born the next day.

Josephus White had taken Anson's birth as a sign they should settle where they were. So he built a homestead—a crude one-room cabin and a barn.

Over time they cleared enough room for some pasture and a few small crops, expanded the cabin and began providing hospitality for travelers from the other wagon trains that followed.

But just when they got things the way they wanted for their little slice of heaven, the unthinkable happened. Josephus died, leaving behind Mrs. White and her three sons. Oscar was twenty-four at the time and Henry twenty, but Anson was only six.

"Your mother was very lucky to have you and Henry after she lost your father," Lily said as the stage rolled along. "I always thought siblings should be close together in age, but with something like that, space is a good thing."

"Yeah," Oscar agreed. "I was already a man and so was Henry, kinda. Anson was just a little tyke. Ma took it the hardest though. Real hard."

"Of course, as would any wife."

But Oscar sighed and faced forward. "You'll see when you meet her."

She was about to ask what he meant, when Willie pulled the team to a stop. "White's Stage Stop!" he called out.

"'Bout time y'got 'ere," someone slurred outside the coach. "Land sakes, Willie, don't make me wait for m'boy 'n 'is new bride!"

"Aw shucks, Mrs. White, I'm right on time," Willie griped as he climbed off his seat. He hopped onto the porch and gave the woman standing there a peck on the cheek. "How's the most beautiful woman in the world?"

"Same as ever. Yer bed's all made up, 'n supper'll be in a couple hours. Now where's m'boy?"

"Right here, Ma." Oscar disembarked from the coach and helped Lily do the same. She looked up at the woman on the porch with a gasp. If Oscar were female, about twenty years older and over a foot shorter, he'd be the spitting image of the woman now descending the porch steps.

Well, except for her lopsided face and smile. Now she understood why Oscar had said his mother took her husband's death hard—the poor dear must've had a stroke. The entire right side of her face looked like it was sliding off the bone. Between that, the single bushy eyebrow across her forehead, and the patchy hair on her face matching that on the top of her head, she made quite the picture.

But Mrs. White's eyes were warm and friendly, her open arms inviting, and she certainly didn't lack for enthusiasm. "There's m'Oscar 'n his new bride!" she slurred, tears in her eyes. She hugged her son first before turning to Lily. "Ooooh, ain't you a vision! Oscar, what a vision she is!"

"I know, Ma. Lily Fair's a beautiful woman. The Lord's been good to me."

"Tha'He has. Now let's hope He's just as good t'yer brothers." She pulled Lily into an embrace that felt like being wrapped in a favorite quilt.

Lily couldn't help but smile and hug her back.

"Hello, Mrs. White. Oscar told me so much about you and Henry and Anson, that I feel I know you already."

"Well, but th'rest o'us dunno ya yet. Might take a while—'em boys o'mine are always busy."

"Working," Oscar quickly tacked on as he took Lily's satchel from Willie. "Anson and Henry are fishing, I expect?"

"Anson's huntin'," his mother corrected. "Dunno where Henry's got to, other'n I know he's fixin' t' surprise his new sister-n-law."

"Me?" Lily said with a smile. "Oh heavens. What does he plan to do?"

"If I knew that, child, 'twouldn't be a surprise. 'N even if I did know, I wouldn't tell ya n'spoil it."

Lily's smile grew. "You're a wise woman, Mrs. White."

"Oh, don't start wi'that 'Mrs. White' nonsense, chile. I'm yer new ma 'n thass whatcha can call me."

Slurred speech or no, her tone said she would brook no argument. "Very well then. Ma, I'm pleased to meet you."

Ma smiled. "'N I been waitin' t'meet ya fer years."

Oscar chuckled and motioned Lily toward the porch steps. "C'mon inside and I'll show ya 'round. Then we'll get to work."

"You will not!" his mother snapped. "You two hain't been married a week—give the poor girl a couple days t'get used t'the place. Or at least 'til tomorra. Ya can hannle the six o'clock stage without'er." She and Oscar had been the only passengers on Willie's stage, but he'd informed her that another one was only a few hours behind theirs. Still, per Ma's order she'd have a chance to unpack and rest.

Oscar laughed. "Anythin' ya say, Ma."

They entered and Lily quickly looked around. It was very obviously a cabin that had been gradually expanded into a sort of hotel. There was a large living room, which also housed the front desk, and a dining room off to the left. Beyond that, a doorway led to a large kitchen.

Ma caught her gaze and waved in that direction. "Kitchen's through there. All th'guest rooms are upstairs, but our bedrooms are down here on th'first floor. When we added th'seconn story, we figgered it best t'keep all o'us in one spot 'n th'guests in another. Works out fine. 'Sides, Henry snores some'n awful."

"Oh, I see," Lily said, trying to hide a smile.

Ma didn't bother to hide hers. "Oscar makes some noise too, fer that matter."

Lily giggled. "Thanks for the warning, but I already know." They'd kept to their own sides of the bed on their wedding night, but Lily had woken once or twice, sure she was hearing the workings of a nearby sawmill. No, it was just Oscar.

"Maybe so, but a man snores loudest in his own bed." Ma winked at her with her good eye.

"Ma!" Oscar complained.

"Well, 's true, ain't it?" his mother said.

Lily managed not to laugh, just. She supposed

she'd have to wait until tonight to find out if Ma was right.

She'd also have to wait and see if Oscar would at last exercise his husbandly rights. So far he hadn't. After their wedding night in Clear Creek, their accommodations didn't lend themselves to any sort of intimacy. Two of the ranches they'd stayed at had only the barn to sleep in. Oscar, being a gentleman, didn't think consummating their marriage with an animal audience looking on was proper.

But tonight would be different—they were home. Not that it was familiar to her, but *she* was home. She'd done nothing but travel since leaving Denver— one night of rest in Clear Creek wasn't enough to compensate for it. But here she was, so she'd better adjust to it. Provided she got the chance. For all she knew, Oscar would send her packing within a few days. Everything came down to what she'd been dreading most.

Once again she looked over the large rooms, the welcoming atmosphere around the hearth, the inviting kitchen beyond. The stage stop was very homey. No wonder people liked to stay there. If she were a weary traveler—which, actually, she was—she'd want to stay there too. And she did want to. But would she get to?

"C'mon, Lily Fair," Oscar said. "I'll show ya our room, then the kitchen. Best room in the whole house."

She couldn't help but laugh. "A true chef if I've ever heard one."

"Tha'he is," his mother agreed. "'N I'm glad he's back. We had a full house lass night, lemme tell ya. Come t'think, I got sheets dryin' on th'line…"

"I can help you with those," Lily offered.

"No need, chile. I'll have 'em folded 'fore supper. Y'just get settled in t'night."

"Thank you… Ma."

Mrs. White nodded. "Glad t'see I gotta daughter that minds. Not insinuatin' nothin', chile. Juss that yer callin' me Ma right off like I asked, warms my heart."

"I'm glad," Lily said.

"Come along, Lily Fair," Oscar said, motioning to a door she hadn't noticed yet, probably because it was on the other side of a huge hutch at one end of the front counter. "This leads to the family bedrooms," he explained as he opened it and stepped through. He pointed to the first door on the left— "That there's Henry's room"—then to the first door on the right a little farther down the hall. "That leads to the kitchen."

"And where is our room?" she asked.

"Third door on the left at the end of the hall. The room opposite is Anson's. Ma's is between ours and Henry's."

"What happens when your brothers get married one day?"

Oscar shrugged. "Then their wives will share their rooms, just like yer gonna share mine."

She shook her head. "I mean, when they have children?"

Oscar stared at her moment, as if startled by the question. "Oh, that. Well, we ain't given that much thought as yet. I guess 'cause everyone figgered I'd be the first to marry."

"Oh," she said with a blush. It was a subject they hadn't covered during the journey from Clear Creek. Her eyes drifted to the floor.

Oscar touched her lightly on the arm to get her attention. "'Course I've thought 'bout children. But I wasn't sure how ya'd feel 'bout them, ya bein' married before and all. I guess ya never had kids with yer first husband…"

"He went off to war before we had a chance," she interrupted.

Oscar stared at her a moment, caught himself and looked away.

Lily wasn't sure what he was thinking. He knew she been married before, even asked a little about John on their journey. But only a little. She put her hand on his arm. "Were you planning on having children?"

"Are children somethin' ya can plan, Lily Fair?" he asked in all honesty.

"Well, to a point," she said after a moment. "Though mostly they're something you hope for."

"Are ya hopin' for some?"

She shrugged, feeling unsure of herself. "I hadn't given it much thought, to be honest. Not at my age…"

"Well, we ain't so old we cain't have none."

"No, we're not." She took a deep breath and let it out slowly. Now that the subject was open, she desperately wanted to close it. "May I see our room?"

"Sure." He walked to the door. "Guess I don't need to carry ya 'cross this threshold."

It was true, but Lily blushed anyway. "You can if you want to."

"If it's all right by you, it's all right by me." He smiled, opened the door and tossed their bags inside, then scooped her up in his arms. "Like I told ya before, I think it's a right romantic notion."

Lily giggled as he carried her into the room and set her on her feet. "It is romantic, now that I think on it."

"Now?" he said in surprise. "I thought on it a lot over the last few years. Maybe more than I should."

"Is that why you sent away for a mail-order bride?" she asked. "Because you thought it would be romantic?"

"One of the reasons, yeah. But also 'cause I knew I'd be the first to get married, I had to think about it long and hard."

"I don't understand."

"I'm the oldest—I gotta set a good example for Henry and Anson. Whatever I do they tend to follow."

"Does that include having children?"

"That includes just about everythin', I reckon."

Lily turned from him, not wanting him to see her face, sense her thoughts. *Would that include sending your bride away after you discovered you didn't want her anymore?* After tonight, she'd probably find out.

"Are ya happy ya married me Lily?"

She was so startled she almost yelped. "Oh, of course I'm happy," she said, perhaps a little too quickly. "If I didn't think this would work, I wouldn't have done it."

He watched her a moment. "Hm," he finally said, then picked up their satchels and put them on the bed. The room was sparse, just a dresser, a large bed with a pretty coverlet, and a trunk resting at the end of the footboard. But it was clean and orderly. The trunk looked like it belonged to a woman—a hope chest, maybe? What was it doing in his room?

As if reading her thoughts, he pointed to it. "Ma thought you might like that."

"Oh," she said in surprise. "She didn't have to give me anything of hers."

"She didn't. I ordered it from Oregon City and had it delivered. She just helped me pick it out."

This time Lily gasped in surprise. "You...you bought it for me?"

"Sure 'nough. I figgered ya'd like somethin' to put stuff in."

Lily glanced around and noted the armoire against the opposite wall. "But it looks like there's plenty of room for what little I have." *More than enough actually*, she thought, looking at her pitiful satchel.

"Not for everyday things," he said. "But for, ya know, heirlooms." He put his hands on his hips and looked at the floor a second or two before adding, "For our children."

Lily felt herself start to sweat. "Of course." Not that there were going to be any—she'd be lucky if she got to stay long enough to put anything in the dresser. In fact, now that she was finally here, she might as well get what she'd been dreading over with. As she saw it, by morning she'd either still be Mrs. Oscar White, or she'd be packing for the next stage elsewhere...

"I'm gonna go help Ma with supper," Oscar said. "The next stage'll be here at six, and it usually has a lotta passengers."

"Where does the six o'clock stage come from?" If she did have to leave the next day, she wanted to know what options she had besides Clear Creek.

"Sometimes from Oregon City headin' to Baker City, sometimes the other way 'round. This bein' Tuesday, it'll be comin' from Baker City."

"And they come through every day?"

"Not every day—depends on the time of year and the weather, and there's no stage on Sundays. We're hopin' one day the train'll come through here."

A hand went to her chest. "But you're nowhere near big enough to handle a train full of people."

"Yet. Someday I hope to build a small hotel."

"A hotel?" She glanced around, even though they were still in his room. "But isn't this already…"

"Nah, still just a stage stop. But I know what yer thinking. Still, if the railroad comes through here, I'd like it to be bigger than what we got now, so we can serve more guests."

"Have the railroad men come here to discuss it with you?" she asked out of curiosity.

"No, but I figger they will one day."

Lily thought of the remote location and wasn't exactly inclined to agree. But Oscar was willing to wait. Which made one of them—she didn't want to wait another night twisting in the winds of fate before she knew if Oscar would be willing to keep her. Her inclination was to just get it over with. But she'd wait until after supper to make her final decision.

Chapter Eight

"...And here's where we keep the flour, sugar and coffee." Oscar pointed at a row of large stone jars. "The rest of it's in a storeroom."

"And where is the storeroom?" Lily Fair asked, curious.

"Off Anson's room."

She gave him a quizzical look. "What?"

"Yeah, that way no one tries to steal anythin' outta it. I'll show ya after supper."

"So you have to go through your brother's room to get to the storeroom?" she asked, still incredulous.

"Yep."

"Poor Anson."

"Aw, he don't mind none. 'Specially since it's his job to see everythin's kept up in the kitchen."

She shrugged. "Well, then I guess I don't have to worry about refilling the flour or sugar, do I?"

"Nope. C'mon, lemme show ya where everythin'

else is." He led her through the kitchen, opening cupboards and drawers, then took her outside to the root cellar.

"Oh my, I've…well, I've…"

"What's the matter?" Oscar asked.

She looked at him in the dim light. "I've never been in a root cellar before."

His eyes popped. "What? Never?"

She shook her head. "I…grew up on a plantation."

Oscar stared at her a moment. He knew she was from the South, knew she'd lost folks in the war, knew her family was on the losing side. But plantation owners? It had never come up, and he hadn't asked. He'd thought her clothing had told him her social status, and they had…but only her current one.

"We had…servants."

"Slaves, ya mean."

Lily Fair hung her head. "Yes." She didn't look up for a while, not until the silence got uncomfortable. "Later it was a few servants, after the slaves were freed." She turned away and walked to the other side of the cellar. "We lost everything, Oscar."

He went to her, put his hands on her shoulders and pulled her close. "I cain't imagine that kinda life."

"It was grand," she said on a sigh. "And it was wrong—I know that now. But at the time, I was a child—it was all I knew. John and I were wed just after South Carolina seceded, just before the war began. Little did we know it was the beginning of the end for us. He enlisted right away and I rarely saw him after that."

"So that's why ya never had children," he replied. She'd spoken in generalities before this. Now he was getting the details.

"Yes. Hard to start a family when you never see your husband."

Oscar gently turned her to face him, never taking his hands off her shoulders. "It ain't gonna be that way between us."

She chuckled nervously. "I should say not. Not out here, where we're the only ones around."

"Not the only ones. Not quite."

She closed her eyes and lowered her head again. "I know, but it's not like I can hitch up the buggy and drive to town either."

"No, it's not," he agreed. "For one, we ain't got a buggy."

She laughed and looked at him.

He cocked his head. "Ya can hitch up a buggy?"

She smiled. "I can."

"Well, ain't ya just full of surprises?" he asked, amused.

"I can ride too."

His eyebrows went up. "Can ya now? If there ain't too many folks on the six o'clock stage, maybe we'll have time to take a ride tomorrow. I'd like to show ya around some. There's a creek 'bout a mile from here where we fish—it's real purty."

She smiled again as her eyes roamed his face.

"What?" he asked, curious as to what she might be thinking.

"You. Such a big strong man, using the word 'pretty.'"

He shrugged. "What of it?"

She laughed again. "I don't know—it seems out of place somehow. Maybe because the men I've met of your size weren't so nice."

"Yeah, I get that a lot. One more reason I like livin' here and doin' what I do. Out here I'm just Oscar, the fella who makes the best rolls in the state. Or, uh, so I'm told," he added with a grin.

To his surprise, she placed her hands over his. They were small and warm, and he liked the feel of them. "Show me what you keep down here."

Holding her hands, he led her to the far wall where they stored the potatoes. He showed her where everything was kept, gave her a brief history of the root cellar and how long it took his father and him to dig it out, then led her outside into the fresh air. By now the sun was fading behind the mountains to the west. "Gonna be dark soon," he commented. "Best I show ya the smokehouse, then we need to go set the table."

"Set the table? But you don't know how many passengers are coming."

"Don't matter. Ma likes the table set. Looks more invitin'."

She nodded her understanding as he headed for the smokehouse. Lily Fair wrinkled her nose as they entered. "Oh my."

"Yeah, the air's pretty gamy in here, but wait'll ya taste some of what I make."

"You? You smoke your own meat?"

"Ain't no one else out here to do it for us. Really, Henry and I both take care of the smokehouse, so I shoulda said 'what *we* make.'"

She waved a dismissive hand. "I know everyone must have their assigned chores. I'm just trying to figure out what mine will be."

"Whatever Ma needs, honey."

Her eyes suddenly flicked to his.

"What is it?"

She shook her head. "Nothing."

She was acting funny, and he detected the same sadness he'd caught when they were in Clear Creek. It came out of nowhere and just as quickly disappeared. Now that he knew a little more about her past, he could understand—maybe she missed her old life. But what could he do about that? This wasn't the South and he sure wasn't some rich plantation owner. If she thought she'd have anything here resembling the life of a Southern belle, she was sadly mistaken.

He led her out of the smokehouse and into the barnyard. "Anson takes care of the barn for the most part, feeds the horses and helps the stage drivers with their stock." His voice had gone flat and he hoped he didn't sound angry. Tarnation, he knew he didn't have a lot, but quite a few women would be more than happy to have what he had. Just his luck to get one that was used to a lot more. Or was she? No sense jumping to conclusions. "Ya said ya lost everything."

"Yes."

"That's why ya went to Denver?"

"Yes, I had an aunt there. But she died and the money…" She looked away. "…well, ran out."

Oscar studied her a moment. "Didn't yer family have money for ya to live on after the war?"

"No," Lily Fair snapped, then shut her eyes as if to erase her reaction. "I'm sorry."

Oscar gave her hand a reassuring squeeze. "I'm just tryin' to understand ya, Lily Fair. That's all."

She glanced at him, the sadness back in her eyes. "When I told you we lost everything, I do mean everything." She looked away again. "More than you know."

"I can see that. But ya don't hafta worry none. Yer my wife and I'm gonna take care of ya from now on."

She slowly raised her face, her lower lip trembling, and nodded.

"Don't cry, Lily Fair. Please don't cry." He put his arms around her. He'd never held her like this before. She felt good wrapped in his arms, her body flush against his. But despite his words and the physical comfort he hoped to give, she still cried. For the life of him, he couldn't figure out why. Maybe the long trip had finally caught up with her. "C'mon, honey, let's get ya into the house. I'll make ya a cup of coffee."

She nodded and sniffed back tears. "I'm sorry, so sorry…"

"No crime in shedding a few tears."

"I know, but…"

"Lily Fair, I understand ya been through a lot."

She gulped and stared at him. Her eyes were big and round and he could see the differing shades of brown and flecks of gold in them.

"Ya lost everythin'," he went on. "I dunno what that's like. The only thing I ever lost was my pa."

She swallowed hard and sniffled some more.

He kept an arm around her as he steered her toward the house. "I know I ain't much…"

"What?!"

Oscar stopped. "Lily Fair, I know I ain't some fancy dude from back east. I'm a simple man."

More sniffles. She wiped her eyes with her hand. "Oscar, there's…something I need to tell you."

He faced her and took her other hand. "What is it?"

She looked at him, trembling. "The war took more than…any of us could imagine."

"I understand that." She was downright shaking, and he pulled her into his arms once more. "Ya don't have to tell me, honey, not if it's gonna upset ya like this." He felt her stiffen and try to pull herself together.

She stepped out of his embrace, as if holding her would push her over the edge. Maybe it would. But maybe it was what she needed. "I know you need to deal with the next stage."

"Well…yeah, I know. But if ya need my help right now…"

Lily Fair shook her head. "I'll be fine, really." She swallowed again and straightened. "Best you get to it, then."

Oscar eyed her carefully. She was doing her best to push her feelings down, but that wasn't going to make whatever was bothering her go away. Still, he wasn't going to force it out of her. She'd tell him when she was ready. "All right, let's go back to the house."

After a short nap, Lily entered the dining room a little before six, just as a man—Henry or Anson?—was pulling silverware out of a drawer in the large hutch. He set the silverware on the table and then hurried out the front door. Lily blinked back the sleep in her eyes and studied the room while wondering where he'd run off to in such a hurry.

The dining table was good-sized and could easily seat eight, ten if they had to. She did notice a couple of extra chairs against one wall, and could guess what they were for.

She was tempted to pitch in and help, then remembered Ma's order and settled for staying out of the way. Maybe she'd offer to wash the supper dishes so Ma could have a little rest. True, she was still tired from the long trip here, but she was also younger and stronger. Surely she and Oscar could handle a batch of dirty dishes—provided Oscar didn't consider it "women's work." But then, he also cooked, so that concept might never occur to him…

Ma entered the room from the kitchen, a vase full of blossoms in it. She set it on the table, then stepped back to admire it. "There now, ain't them purty?"

"Are those cherry blossoms?" Lily asked.

"Sure are. Make a nice centerpiece, don't they?"

Lily smiled. "Yes, they do." She yawned, much to her embarrassment.

"You 'n Oscar best make it an early night," Ma commented.

Lily rubbed her face. "I'm terribly sorry, I didn't mean to do that."

"Cain't he'p but yawn if ya need to, chile."

"We can turn in after we clean up the supper dishes…"

"Nah, nah, you two go t'bed after ya eat."

"Please, I insist," Lily said. Besides, the longer she waited to get to bed, the more likely Oscar would simply fall asleep instead of exercising his husbandly rights. She'd almost told him about her hardship, but couldn't get the words out. Thankfully, he'd said she didn't have to and, coward that she was, she didn't argue. But she couldn't put him off forever, and she'd already decided she needed to tell him now, before she got too attached to his family or the stage stop.

A man barged through the front door, a string of fish in his hand, but Lily didn't think it was the man she saw before. "Look, Ma! I done got supper!"

Ma sighed in relief. "'Bout time ya got back, Henry. Well, don't juss stan' there, go clean 'em. Oh, by th'way, meet yer new sister-in-law, Lily."

Henry turned to face her with a huge smile. He looked like a younger version of Oscar, only smaller and with lighter hair. But he had the same dark eyes and single eyebrow—that seemed to be a family trait. "Hi, I'm Henry!"

Lily smiled back, unsure what to do. Henry was a full-grown man, yet something about him…aside from what Oscar had shared.

"I got ya a surprise!"

Lily glanced at his mother, who stood behind him, a warm smile on her face. "You…you did?"

"Sure did! I'll go fetch it for ya! I done hid it out in the barn!" He took off, the string of fish still in his hand.

"Henry!" his mother cried after him.

"Oh yeah—forgot!" Henry made a sharp turn just as he reached the front door, making a bee-line for the kitchen instead.

"Y'hafta 'scuse Henry—he gets hisself all worked up. He's been workin' on yer present fer weeks."

"My…present?"

"A weddin' present. It's fer both you'n Oscar, but mainly for you."

Lily smiled. "How sweet." Inwardly she cringed. This would make having to leave (if *you have to leave*, she reminded herself) all the harder.

She watched Henry run out of the kitchen, across the living/dining area and out the front door without a word, and couldn't help but laugh.

"Be careful 'bout laughin' 'round Henry," Ma warned. "He gets sens'tive 'bout it sometimes."

Lily nodded in understanding, glad that Oscar had already told her a little about his "special" younger brother.

A minute later, Henry returned. "Come and see, Lily!"

She glanced at Ma, who nodded encouragingly, and followed Henry out to the porch.

He danced around a lovely handmade rocking chair, smiling jovially. "Here it is! What do ya think?"

Lily gasped. "Oh, Henry, it's beautiful! You made this all by yourself?"

"Sure did. I like makin' things."

Ma had joined them by now. "He's quite the furniture maker. Got inta it 'bout six years ago—makes all kindsa things. He made the chairs, and th'dinin' table—one we usta have was purt near collapsin'. Thass what got him goin'."

Lily walked around her present. There were no elaborate carvings on it, nothing fancy, but it was shapely and sturdy. Obviously Henry took great pride in his work. "Thank you, Henry." She gave him a quick kiss on the cheek.

Henry blushed almost purple. "Aw gee…wasn't nothin'." He gave her another wide grin. "I can make ya anythin' ya want!"

"I'm sure you can." She smiled and sat in the

chair, rocking experimentally a few times. "Oh, Henry, this *is* nice."

"Be nicer once Ma makes a cushion for it—ain't that right, Ma?"

"Yep. Awready started on it."

Lily glanced between them. "You two shouldn't have gone to all this trouble."

"Ain't no trouble when it's fer family," Ma said. "Now, Henry, go clean yer fish."

Henry fidgeted as he teetered between staying on the porch and doing what his mother said. "I'm glad ya like it," he finally said, then went inside.

Lily ran her hands over the smooth arms of her present. "He is very talented."

"Yeah, he is. Henry might be differ'nt from other folks, but he ain't without skills."

"I can see that." Lily stood. "Where shall I put it?"

"Ya can leave it on th'porch if ya like, or I can have Oscar take it t'yer room."

"No." She gazed out at the barnyard. "I think I like it right here."

"Juss know that if ya leave it on th'porch, the guests'll use it."

"Oh, I forgot about that." Lily's mind had been too fixed on speaking with Oscar later. Maybe she should try to focus on something else for a while. "I'll have to think about it. Ma, would you show me how you cook fish?"

"'Course, chile. Follow me."

Chapter Nine

As it turned out, there were only three passengers on the six o'clock stage. Abe the stagecoach driver was a squat little man with bright blue eyes and a chipper demeanor. He scurried around like a squirrel searching for nuts. Oscar told her that in the morning Abe would take his charges as far as Oregon City, after which any going farther would transfer to other stages heading north or south. Abe, in turn, would take on eastbound passengers and be back at the Whites' by Saturday.

Abe's passengers were a Mr. and Mrs. Truitt and a lawyer named Maas, a tall, dour man who said very little at supper. Mrs. Truitt more than made up for it. "Newlyweds! Oh, how wonderful! And you were married only last week too." She turned to her husband. "Isn't that romantic, George?"

Mr. Truitt, a portly man with salt-and-pepper hair

and brown eyes, mumbled "mm-hmm" at his trout and potatoes before taking another bite.

"Was it a big wedding?" Mrs. Truitt asked.

"Not very." Lily glanced at Oscar, who had a mouthful of food and couldn't answer. "Just the preacher and his wife and a few…er…guests."

Oscar suppressed a chuckle. Their last-minute wedding guests had been a topic of conversation for hours during her stage ride home. He'd entertained her with wild stories of the Cookes, Dunnigans, Wallers and more, half of which she chalked up as tall tales. She wondered if he'd tell the same stories to the new arrivals after supper.

"Are ya visitin' folks in Oregon City?" Ma asked Mrs. Truitt.

"Our daughter just had her third child. She married a banker there. They do quite well."

"Thass nice," Ma slurred.

Lily noticed Mr. Maas cringe in response to her new mother-in-law's speech. All things considered, the woman was fortunate to be able to speak at all. "How about you, Mr. Maas? Do you have relatives in Oregon City?"

"No," was his gruff response. "I am headed to Salem. I have business to attend there."

"Really?" Mrs. Truitt enthused. "Are you a political man, to have business in the capital?"

"Something of that nature," Mr. Maas responded in a way that indicated he wasn't inclined to talk about it.

The rest of the meal continued in relative quiet, once Mrs. Truitt finally got around to eating instead of talking. Once everyone had finished, Oscar and his mother excused themselves to get the dessert and coffee, leaving Lily to entertain the guests. Anson had yet to appear and Henry, having come in late after getting Abe's team taken care of, ate his supper in the kitchen, then went to tend the family's stock.

"My, but your husband certainly is a large fellow, isn't he?" Mrs. Truitt commented after Oscar disappeared into the kitchen.

"Yes." Lily forced a smile. "He certainly is."

"I wonder if your children will be as tall—that is, if you're going to have any."

George Truitt cleared his throat loud enough to make everyone jump in their seats. "Martha dear, we've talked about your prying into others' affairs," he said more softly, but with an undertone of restrained anger. "It's none of our business if they're going to have children or not. Keep your nose out of it."

Oscar was in the room so fast that Lily didn't even notice how he got there. It was as if he'd appeared out of thin air at her side. "Is there a problem?" he asked in his deep voice.

Martha Truitt had gone pale. "None whatsoever. You've nothing to worry about, sir." She glanced at her husband as if he were a volcano about to erupt.

Oscar eyed them both, then looked at Lily. "Everythin' all right?"

"Of course. Just a…difference of opinion."

"You'll have to forgive Martha—she, erm, is still learning caution," George replied. At the moment, Martha seemed to be memorizing the grain of the wood on the table.

Lily waved Oscar back toward the kitchen. "It's nothing. Everything's fine." In fact, she really didn't want him to leave—his protectiveness was making her feel like she hadn't since John went off to fight with the Confederates.

"If you're sure." Oscar didn't sound convinced.

"I am," she said gently, smiling for added effect. It worked—Oscar slowly turned and retreated back to the kitchen.

"My heavens," Martha said, finally finding her voice. "I wouldn't want to be in an argument with your husband, Mrs. White. Why, the damage a man of that size could do to a body…"

"Martha…" George warned.

"I…I was just saying…"

Now George's voice dropped to a hiss. "And we know what happened in Laramie because you were 'just saying.' And in Omaha, and in St. Louis, and in Cairo. You can't go on like this—it is *not* proper…" His voice was starting to rise, but he caught himself and looked around the table. "My apologies."

Mr. Maas tried to take a compromising position. "I would think a man of Mr. White's size and build is used to being noticed."

"Indeed," agreed Lily. "Most men of his stature

are often challenged by others. Usually men who think they have something to prove."

Mr. Maas nodded and scooped up his last bite of potatoes. "Pity the man who thinks that. I have heard about your husband along the route—but mainly that he is one of the finest cooks in the West."

Lily laughed. "I've heard that too, but I have yet to try any of his cooking. His mother and I fried the trout. I hope you liked it."

"It was wonderful," Martha Truitt said, more carefully now.

"Excellent potatoes and vegetables as well," her husband put in. He looked up as Ma entered the room, a pie in each hand. "Ah, dessert at last."

"And coffee," Oscar declared as he followed his mother, holding a tray. He set it on the table, removed the coffee pot, cups and saucers and began to pour as Ma sliced up the pies. Soon everyone had their cup and a slice and dug in.

"Mrs. White," George said, "this has to be the best apple pie I've ever had."

"Thank you," Ma said. "But it's Oscar's recipe."

"It's delicious," Martha agreed. "I don't suppose you'd share it."

"No, I don't suppose I would," Oscar said with a grin. "Otherwise you might not come back."

"Well, we have to go home, so of course we'll be back," she said with a smile. "But I understand— family secret and all." She glanced at her husband, who smiled as if to say *much better.*

Lily smiled too, in relief that the Truitts weren't about to be at loggerheads again. "Well, perhaps we can send you off with a pie when you come through again." She quickly looked at Oscar, hoping she hadn't overstepped her bounds. "If that's all right?"

Oscar shrugged. "That might be agreeable, if we have a pie to spare."

"Why, that would be lovely!" Martha exclaimed. "Thank you for your generosity."

Lily was just glad she hadn't made Oscar angry—it was the last thing she wanted to do right now. Soon dessert would be over and once they did the dishes they'd retire for the evening. And then...

After the gentlemen each had a second helping of pie, Lily helped Oscar clear the table and let Ma entertain the passengers while they saw to the kitchen. Willie and Abe had come in after checking on their teams and were now eating their own suppers on the porch. "Food's great as always, Oscar," Willie said. "Ain't seen Anson 'round, though—where is the boy?"

"Not sure," he said, unconcerned. "Probably out huntin' rabbits. Don't worry, he'll turn up."

Lily was curious about Anson and hoped she'd get to actually meet him before she and Oscar went to their room. For all she knew she'd be leaving on one of the stages in the morning. She watched her new husband stack dishes in the dry sink, then took a bucket from underneath it and went outside to the pump. She knew this task—one of the few she'd performed at her aunt's.

He came back inside, set the bucket on the stove and continued to tidy the kitchen as the water heated. Lily watched in fascination as he put some things away and set others up to make the next day's breakfast preparations go easier. He checked the water on the stove and, with a nod, poured some into a metal tub he placed in the dry sink. "What would you like me to do?" she asked.

"I'll wash, you dry?" He handed her a dishrag.

It didn't take long to blow through the piles, even with Willie and Abe's plates coming in halfway through. Before Lily knew it, Oscar was steering her toward the door on the other side of the kitchen. This meant they were going to their room…

In a panic, she stopped just short of the bedroom door. "I…I'd like a glass of water." She cringed at the lame comment—as if a quick drink would buy her any time or make her task any easier.

"'Course, I'll fetch one for ya. Go 'head and get into yer bedclothes."

Lily's eyes widened. But then, if she could get into her bedclothes before he returned with her water, she might have a chance to put off dealing with the issue until tomorrow. After all, she'd managed to change while he wasn't in the room—or in some cases, the barn—their entire time together. What was one more night? And he did look very tired. She *should* wait to tell him, shouldn't she? Maybe tomorrow night…

"Ya know, after I get your water, I oughta go look for Anson," Oscar mused. "He shoulda been back by now, rabbits or no rabbits."

Lily jumped at the lifeline he unwittingly offered. "Oh, er…yes, yes!"

Oscar cocked his head to one side. "Ya sure there ain't nothin' the matter?"

"Oh yes, I'm sure. I'll just go crawl in bed." She faked a yawn. "I am mighty tired."

He nodded. "Me too. But I better make sure my brother's all right. Ain't like him to be gone this far past suppertime."

Lily sobered. "Should I come with you?" she said without thinking, her concern for Oscar's brother momentarily pushing aside her fears.

"Nah, honey, you stay here. Go to bed and get some sleep."

Lily's shoulders slumped in relief as soon as he left. She felt guilty about taking advantage of his absent brother, but one more night couldn't hurt. Besides, she liked the stage stop and could easily see what life might be like if she were able to stay. Still, she knew she was only postponing the inevitable. At some point, she'd have to tell him—and show him—everything.

Oscar held the lantern higher and peered into the woods around him. "Anson!" he called, hand cupped at the side of his mouth. He'd been yelling his brother's name for the last twenty minutes, to no avail. He was also armed, given that you never knew what you might run into in the wilderness surrounding the stage stop.

Finally he heard someone crashing through the woods. Anson emerged, a string of rabbits in one hand. "Land sakes, brother, yer gonna scare all the game away," he hissed.

"Not with all the noise yer makin'," Oscar complained. "Where ya been all this time?"

"Checkin' my snares. Ya know how long that takes."

Oscar sighed and shook his head. "Yeah, but that don't keep us from worryin' when yer out past dark!"

"I'm sorry, Oscar—I didn't mean to frighten no one." Anson went to his big brother and gave him a hug. "Glad to have you back." He stepped away and smiled. "So yer hitched?"

Oscar nodded. "Yes, I am."

"Well," Anson said with excitement, "what's it like?"

Oscar shrugged. "Well…it's kinda like havin' a new friend follow ya 'round all day. Ya talk to them, try to get to know them better. I suppose it'd be different if we'd had time to court beforehand."

Anson laughed. "Is she purty?"

"What, ya ain't even seen her?"

"Nah—I was only in the house a few minutes today. Just long 'nough to set the table, so Ma didn't get mad."

Oscar nodded and smiled. "Yeah, she's real purty."

Anson punched the air. "Woo-ee! My big brother's married! I cain't hardly believe it. She a good cook?"

"Well, that's what's ya might call the down side. She says she don't cook much."

Anson's happy countenance fell. "Can ya teach her?"

"'Course I can teach her. Lily Fair's smart. I plan to teach her a lot."

"Lily Fair—that's sure a purty name," Anson sighed, then eyed his rabbits. "Maybe she can start with these."

Oscar smiled. "Good idea, little brother. Tomorrow I'll teach her how to make rabbit stew."

Anson laughed. "She gotta learn sometime." He suddenly sobered and kicked the ground a few times. "Ya see any folks we know in Clear Creek?"

"Just about everyone. Heck, the Cooke brothers and their wives were at my weddin' along with Mr. and Mrs. Van Cleet, the Dunnigans, the Mulligans…"

"The Turners?" Anson asked hopefully.

"No, didn't see any of the Turners."

Anson kicked the ground again. "Not one?"

Oscar grinned. "You mean, did I see *Emeline*?"

Even in the dim lantern light he could see his brother blush. "Yeah, Emeline. Ya didn't see her at all?"

"'Fraid not. Maybe next time we go to town, ya can come along."

"But what about Ma and Henry? They cain't manage this place by themselves."

"They could if they had to. Worse comes to worse, though, I could leave Lily Fair behind to help…but I'd rather not." At this point, he was thinking aloud. He could leave Lily Fair with them to help with the chores, once she'd settled in and he'd taught her a few things. But he knew she'd need to go back to Clear Creek and visit with the other women sometimes. Besides, he more or less promised she'd come along on the next trip.

But he also knew his younger brother was sweet on Emeline Turner. She'd come through the stage stop a few times when she helped her parents move to Oregon City months before. Their plan was for her and her brother Eli to run the family farm together and send their folks money to live on. Mr. Turner's health was bad and Doc Waller had suggested city living might be better for him. There was talk that Tom, the eldest Turner and a deputy sheriff up in the town of Nowhere in the Washington Territory, might return to Clear Creek with his wife Rose and their daughter Hannah to work the farm. But nothing had been settled yet, so it was all up in the air.

"When ya think yer gonna go back to Clear Creek?" Anson pressed.

"Gonna be a while. But Lily plans to write to Belle and Sadie Cooke. Maybe ya wanna send a letter along with hers?"

"To Belle and Sadie?"

Oscar laughed. "No, ya dumb cluck—to Emeline!"

"Emeline! I cain't do that!"

"Why not? It's just a letter, not a marriage proposal. Ya like her, don't ya?"

Anson went crimson. "Who said anything about…?"

"Oh, c'mon," Oscar said as he turned toward home. "Ya been moonin' over her since she came through here with her folks. What's wrong with writin' her a note?"

Anson was speechless. "But…but what if she don't feel the same?"

"Then you'll find out sooner, and ya won't waste time on someone who ain't set her cap for ya. And if she *does* feel the same, you'll know that."

Anson took off his hat, crushed it under his arm and ran his hand through his hair. "I dunno…"

Oscar stopped, frustrated. "If I can send away for a mail-order bride and marry a woman I ain't never seen before, ya can write Emeline Turner a note to say howdy."

Anson's eyes were wide. "But…what should I say?"

"Don't worry 'bout that right now. Just decide yer gonna do it."

Anson's brow furrowed. "Decidin's hard sometimes."

"Ain't nothin' to it. Look at me, I decided to up and get married."

Anson nodded, looking sick. "But you're older and braver than I am."

"Older, maybe. I ain't so sure about braver—ya don't see me checkin' rabbit snares after dark."

Anson chuckled. "So do ya like bein' married?"

That caught Oscar off guard. "Well..."

"Really? Ya gotta think 'bout it?"

"Well, heck, it's only been a few days. We barely know each other."

Anson nodded and sighed. "Man, I wanna get married."

Oscar raised an eyebrow. "I know. Now let's get on home—Ma's probably worried by now, and we got three guests in on the six o'clock. Tomorrow I'll introduce ya to Lily Fair. Maybe she can help ya write yer note to Emeline."

Anson's face lit up at the suggestion. "I never thought of that. She's from where?"

"Charleston, South Carolina. A real big-city Southern lady."

Anson's eyes grew wider still. "Gosh, Oscar. Yer one lucky man."

Oscar smiled and glanced up at the star-filled sky. "I guess I am, ain't I?" But he still had so many questions about Lily Fair. And she didn't seem eager to give him answers.

Chapter Ten

When Lily awoke the next morning, Oscar was already up and working in the kitchen. At least she assumed that's where he was. Judging from the wonderful smells wafting into the room, it seemed a good bet. She got out of bed, dressed, ran a brush through her hair and hastily pinned it up, then hurried out to join him. "Why didn't you wake me?" she asked as she arrived.

Oscar was pulling a sheet of biscuits out of the oven. "Well, Lily Fair, ya looked so purty and peaceful sleepin' there. I didn't have the heart to disturb ya."

Her own heart melted at his words—how considerate! "Thank you, that was very kind. I was tired." More than she'd realized—she'd fallen asleep the moment her head hit the pillow. She hadn't even heard him come in, nor woken up when he'd crawled into bed.

"Would ya mind settin' the table for breakfast?" Oscar asked.

"Not at all. Do you want me to use the same silverware we had last night?"

"Yep. We're not fancy here."

She blinked a few times. "Oh, I didn't mean to imply..."

"I know," he cut in. "I just wanted ya to know we use the same silver and whatnot for everythin'."

She nodded and left the kitchen. He must have been thinking about what she'd told him the night before, about growing up on a plantation with slaves and money. Oh yes, at one time they'd had plenty of both. But as her father used to tell her, nothing lasts forever. How true that was.

She went to the hutch, took out silverware for ten—though she wasn't sure if Willie and Abe would join them at the table—and set it out, then did the same with plates, bowls, cups, saucers and whatever else she thought Oscar might want. Once she was done, she returned to the kitchen. "Anything else I can do?"

"Here." He handed her a huge tray laden with fresh biscuits. "Go 'head and put these on the table. I'll bring the bacon in next. The drivers'll be comin' downstairs any minute. Oh, and when ya come back, take the coffee pot and pour a cup for everyone. Thanks."

Lily smiled. Oscar could run his own restaurant, probably anywhere he wanted. Hmm, maybe that wasn't such a bad idea. But look at what he was already doing—and without having to leave the home he clearly loved.

She shrugged at her thoughts, took the biscuits into the other room and set them on the table, went back for the pot of coffee and filled each cup. She stepped back and admired her first work of the day. She'd set the right number of places, provided the drivers joined them inside (Oscar had just implied they would—lucky break there) and no new passengers had come in overnight.

Maybe one had—she saw a handsome young man descending the stairs into the main living room and recognized him as the man who was getting the silver out the evening before. This had to be Anson, the youngest brother.

"Well, lookie here," he said happily. "Ya must be Lily Fair, my new sister!"

Wait a minute—did he say "sister"? Did they already consider her family? Oh dear—if it turned out Oscar didn't want her, this would make things even more difficult. "Um, yes, I suppose I am. And you must be Anson."

"Sure am—howdy!" He held out his hand.

Lily stared at it a moment before she gave it a shake. "Pleased to meet you. And you can just call me Lily." Oscar called her "Lily Fair," and something in her wanted to reserve that for him alone.

Anson stepped back, hands on hips. "Last night

Oscar told me ya were purty, but he wasn't tellin' the half of it. Yer beautiful."

Lily blushed. "Why, thank you." She quickly looked him over. He was about the same height as Henry, but not as broad. He was also probably the best-looking of the bunch—even his distinctive White eyebrow had a little more separation in the middle. And where Oscar and Henry's faces were round, Anson's was more angular, chiseled, more classically handsome.

She wasn't the only one who thought so either. "Mornin', Handsome Anson!" Willie said as he bounded down the stairs. "Missed ya at supper last night—good huntin', I take it?"

"Not huntin', really—just checking my snares. Took longer than usual, though, 'cause the catch was good."

"I unnerstand, though I ain't trapped nothin' in quite a spell. Abe traps and hunts now and then, but our schedules keep us awful busy these days."

Anson laughed. "I know. That's one reason I'll never be a stagecoach driver."

Willie smacked him on the back, then turned to Lily. "What's for breakfast, Mrs. White?"

She swept a hand toward the table. "Well, the biscuits are done, and I do believe bacon is on the way. You'll have to ask Oscar what else he has planned."

"Woo-ee!" Willie exclaimed and clapped his hands together in anticipation. "That means there's fried taters and eggs a-comin'."

Anson saw Lily's confusion. "Oscar and Ma have this schedule—they make certain breakfasts on certain days one week, then switch the meals the next week so the drivers don't get the same breakfast every time they come through."

"I like it," Willie said as he took a seat and patted his belly. "Variety."

Anson sat next to him. "Speakin' of which, we're havin' rabbit stew tonight. Too bad yer gonna miss it."

Willie's face fell. "Dagnabit! I would hafta leave this mornin'. Rotten luck…"

Anson made a show of looking up and down the table like he was surveying it for a sumptuous banquet instead of a country breakfast. "Better luck next time, Willie."

Willie shook his head in dismay and reached for his cup of coffee. "Well, them's the breaks. Maybe next time."

Lily, still standing off to the side, started to worry. She'd never had rabbit stew before—fricassee, yes, and jugged rabbit once, but surely not what her new brother-in-law was talking about. Would she be expected to help prepare it? Could she?

Anson must've caught the look on her face. He laughed and reached for a biscuit. "Don't worry, I already skinned and cleaned them and gave them to Oscar."

Her eyes widened. "You did?" Her mind raced—

had she seen a stew pot on the stove? She couldn't recall.

"I cain't wait to see what sorta stuff yer gonna cook up, Mrs. White," Willie said with a smile, showing missing teeth.

She smiled back weakly. "Neither can I. I'm afraid I'm not a very experienced cook. But Oscar says he'll teach me." *If I last that long...*

"Then yer a very lucky lady." Willie reached for a biscuit too, but stopped and looked at Anson. "Yer brother ain't gonna come out here and hit me with a spoon or somethin' if I take one, is he?"

"I took one," Anson pointed out.

"Yeah, but ya live here—he needs ya to tend stock and suchlike. Me, I might be expandable."

Lily laughed. "Whatever are you two talking about?"

"No laughin' matter, ma'am," Willie said. "Oscar don't like nobody startin' eatin' 'fore the meal's all ready. Sometimes he'll cut some slack, but ya never know when."

Her eyes widened in disbelief. Just what sort of sentence did her husband pass when it came to roll-snatching?

"It ain't as bad as all that," Anson argued. "Here, Willie, take a biscuit. I'll testify in your defense." Willie chuckled as he took it, then reached for the crock of butter.

Unsure what to do next, Lily took the coffee pot

back to the kitchen and set it on the stove. "I just met Anson," she commented.

"Yeah, he got in too late last night to say hi," Oscar said. "Sorry 'bout that."

I'm not, she thought—it had let her stall one more day. Then she chided herself: *No, stop. You don't know what's going to happen—maybe he won't mind them. How can you know until he sees for himself?* That was the problem—there was no other way of knowing. And her whole life rested on it.

"Sleep well, chile?" Ma asked as she entered the kitchen.

Lily spun at the sound of Ma's voice and almost tripped over her own feet. "Oh dear, I'm sorry."

Ma raised her eyebrow at her—on the good side of her face, anyway. "A li'l jumpy this mornin'. Not enough sleep?"

"She slept like a rock," Oscar answered before she could. "Didn't even wake up when I went to bed." He handed Lily a plate of eggs. "Can ya manage?"

"Of course." She hurried out of the kitchen, her face red with embarrassment. She *was* jumpy. If she'd been smart, she'd have waited up for Oscar and told him everything, gotten it over with. Now she had another entire day to worry about it and perhaps balk again, and what good would that do? *Lily, you are such a silly woman*, she thought as she set down the eggs and nervously wiped her hands on her skirt.

Ma followed with a plateful of bacon, then Oscar with a big pan of fried potatoes and onions, and finally Henry carrying a pitcher of cream and a bowl of blackberries. Lily couldn't believe the amount of food he'd made, even though they were feeding ten people. The Whites might not be rich, but they—and their guests—ate like kings. After all those weeks of near-starvation, she appreciated that.

The passengers came down the stairs and joined them at the table. "Smells fine, Mrs. White," Mr. Maas commented almost grudgingly. "I must be sure to stop here again when I travel."

"That's why we do it," Ma said. "How d'ya think Oscar got t'be such a good cook?"

The lawyer looked at Oscar. "This is your work, sir? Well, I am impressed. I imagine the animal side of me will be quite happy after this repast. It's too bad I must move on."

Oscar didn't turn a hair. "Glad to be of service, sir. I do like to experiment a little."

"I used to like to experiment with my cooking," said Martha Truitt. "But it never worked out."

George Truitt sat next to her. "But your *non*-experiments certainly do." He patted his ample belly, and everyone laughed. Lily included, though she was mostly happy to see they weren't bickering. She still wondered what trouble Martha's loose tongue had caused in all those places her husband had mentioned, but decided she was better off not knowing. She knew better than to ask anyway.

Ma said a quick blessing, and as soon as everyone said "Amen" reached for the bacon. Lily was surprised her prayer wasn't longer—maybe she reserved those for when it was only family. Oscar had warned her that Ma's mealtime prayers could get long, and embarrassing. When it came to speaking with the Almighty, she didn't hold back. Maybe it was a good thing there were guests at the stage stop right now.

"What're ya'n Lily gonna do today, son?" Ma asked.

Oscar was spooning potatoes onto his plate. "After we clean up the kitchen, I thought I'd show her the creek and a few other places." He looked at Willie. "Yer gonna be back in two days?"

Willie nodded as he chewed and swallowed. "Good Lord willin' and the creek don't rise."

Oscar turned to Lily. "If you want to write Belle or Sadie or the other womenfolk a letter, you can send it back to Clear Creek with Willie when he comes through again."

She stopped eating and stared at her plate. "I would like to send them a thank you note for the wedding present they gave us."

Oscar smiled and surprised her with a wink. "Yeah, I think I'd like to add a few words when ya write it. Remind me, will ya?"

"Weddin' present?" Henry asked innocently.

"I'll tell ya later." Oscar continued to eat.

Lily's eyes darted around the table and watched everyone enjoy the fine meal. Her eyes then drifted up the staircase. She hadn't seen that part of the house yet, but she sure liked what she had seen. She had a brief vision of sitting on the front porch in the chair Henry made for her, rocking back and forth on a warm summer evening, Oscar in a chair beside her, their baby sleeping contentedly in her lap…

Oh please, Lord, let that be so, she prayed in silent anguish. *I like my new family. I know I've only been here less than a day, but I don't think I could bear to leave. Please, have Oscar let me stay.*

Two hours later Lily stood next to Oscar in one of the most beautiful, tranquil spots she'd ever seen. A small creek ran through a grassy area with an odd mix of maple, alder, pine and cedar trees. "Who planted these?" she asked.

"Pa planted the alder," Oscar told her. "We think someone else might've planted the maple—don't know if they were settlers, Injuns or what. Probably the same folks that built the dam, though. The pines have been here all along."

She studied the deep pool that had been formed by the little log dam, perfect for swimming. It was ringed with grass, the various trees and lots and lots of daffodils. She took a deep breath of the sweet air, enjoying the sound of the water as it flowed over the top of the dam. "Whoever it was, they created something lovely. Like something out of a dream."

"They certainly did." He put an arm around her, and she stiffened slightly, then forced herself to relax. She didn't want him to think she didn't like him touching her, because she did—his hold was comforting, even more so in this setting. She felt like she could stand there with him, stare into the pool and listen to the birds sing forever.

"I come here to think," he continued. "I think a lot here. Made up my mind about ya in this very spot."

Feeling bold, she leaned into him and rested her head against his shoulder. "I like it here."

"Everyone does. One reason we don't show this place to folks. Call it selfish, but we like to keep it to ourselves."

She smiled to herself. Now that she'd seen it, she wasn't going to mention the spot to any of the passengers that came through either. "You said you made up your mind about me here?"

"Yep. Prayed real hard about it."

She chewed on her lower lip a few times. Now was as good a time as any. "And are you…happy with how the Lord answered that prayer?"

He looked at her, studied her face, then kissed the top of her head. "Sure am. Hope you are too."

She swallowed hard, his words cracking the callus around her heart. She closed her eyes, relishing the warmth that spread through her body. "Yes, I am."

Oscar smiled and turned to face her. He traced a path from her cheek to her chin with his finger. "Yer skin's so soft. So purty."

Despite her nerves, she smiled. "Thank you."

He chuckled. "Ya sound like I just complimented ya on a new hat."

Her smile broadened with embarrassment. "I'm sorry... I..."

"Shhh. Don't talk, Lily Fair."

She blinked at him, not understanding why he wanted her to be quiet.

She quickly found out. The kiss was soft, gentle—and the first since their wedding. When she'd been so caught up with worry over what would happen when they finally got around to consummating their marriage, she'd never considered the kissing part. Granted, once he got a good look at her, *all* of her, she didn't know if he'd want to...

Oscar's other arm wrapped around her, and she reveled in the strong embrace. He was like a shelter, a protection against the world, a safe haven she'd never want to leave. But would she have to regardless? She didn't want to, didn't even want this kiss to stop. Wasn't it her right as his wife to enjoy this small slice of pleasure, even if it disappeared in an instant?

Granted, she might be worried about nothing—perhaps he would accept her as she was and not send her away. But if there was one thing she'd learned from the war, it was to never assume. She had to be ready for the worst. And if that happened...well, Oscar was a gentleman, so he'd probably pay her stage fare back to Clear Creek. Then she could ask Mr. Van Cleet for a job in his hotel. He seemed a kindly man, and had mentioned at the wedding supper that he'd have to hire more folks soon. Yes, that would be her plan...

Oscar broke the kiss and gazed into her eyes. "Hello there, Mrs. White."

Lily couldn't help but smile. "Hello, Mr. White," she whispered.

He glanced at the smooth surface of the pool. "Too bad it ain't a lot warmer. We could go swimmin'."

"Brrrr." She shivered. "I expect it won't be warm enough for that for months."

He nodded. "But there are other things that are."

She blushed, then pulled her arms from between them and wrapped them around his waist.

"That feels mighty nice, Lily Fair."

"I'm glad."

He rested his cheek on the top of her head as they gazed at the water. "Ya make me feel good, honey. Real good."

Lily shut her eyes tight, bracing herself. "Oscar... I need to tell you something."

Chapter Eleven

"What is it?" he asked, pulling back a little.

Lily looked into his eyes and saw curiosity mixed with concern. "I should've told you this before we got married. But I wasn't sure how you would react." She heard the fear in her voice and wondered if Oscar heard it as well.

He did, if his creased brow was any hint. "Told me what, Lily Fair?"

She took a deep breath, then another, as if readying herself to jump in the water. "I'd tell you to sit down for this, but there doesn't seem to be anywhere to do so," she said, faking a laugh.

Oscar took her hand, walked several steps to his right where the grass was thicker, and pulled her down to sit next to him. "We're sittin' now, so go 'head."

Leave it to Oscar to be so practical. She plucked

a few blades of grass and tore them apart, suddenly unable to form words.

Oscar put a hand over hers to still her fidgeting. "Go on, honey, it's all right. Whatever it is ya gotta say, just spit it out." He cocked his head to one side. "Ya ain't 'fraid I'll get mad, are ya?"

She spoke before she could think. "I'm afraid you'll put me on the next stage back to Clear Creek!" Then she burst into tears.

Oscar immediately drew her into his arms. "C'mon now, Lily Fair, it cain't be as bad as all that. Can it?"

She nodded reluctantly. "I'm afraid it can," she managed between sobs.

Oscar tucked a finger under her chin, raised her face to his and kissed her gently. Then he playfully rubbed her nose with his. "Tell me, honey, what's botherin' ya? I dunno what it is, but somethin's been makin' ya sad since we were in Clear Creek."

His words and actions so stunned her that she forgot to keep crying. "I…I'm sorry. I don't want to be a bother or worry to you, but if I don't tell you about this and let you make up your mind, then I'm going to drive myself mad."

"What do ya mean, make up my mind? 'Bout what?"

Lily took a deep breath, sat up straight, pulled up the right sleeve of her dress as far as it would go and twisted her arm around. "About this."

As she expected, Oscar's eyes went round as saucers. From the elbow up past her sleeve were horrible red scars, forming an ugly pattern over her skin like wax melted down the side of a candle. "Lily Fair, what happened?"

Lily's heart warmed at the concern in his voice. But would that be enough? Somehow she doubted it. "Back in '65, Sherman's army reached Charleston and the surrounding area. They took everything they could carry, then they burned our plantation to the ground. My mother-in-law was there too, and…" She started to sob again.

Oscar pulled her onto his lap to cradle her in his arms. "Hush now, darlin', it's all right. Ya don't hafta cry. I know it musta been terrible for ya, but it's just some scars. Ya didn't think that was gonna bother me, did ya?" He leaned to one side and pulled a handkerchief out of his pocket. "Here, honey, wipe them tears."

His voice was so soft, so deep and gentle, that it made Lily cry harder. He truly cared for her, she could hear it, feel it and wanted it. But what would he do when he saw the rest? "It's…not just *some* scars, Oscar. It's not just my arm…"

"It's all right—"

"No, you don't understand!" she wailed. "I'm covered with them! I tried to rescue my mother-in-law and, and I couldn't save her. But my dress caught on fire, and my shoes. My legs, my back, my…my breasts. Everywhere from my shoulders down, except my hands and forearms. They're all over…"

Oscar stared at her in open-mouthed shock, and

she braced herself for the inevitable. He would tell her he didn't want her anymore…

But he didn't. Instead he slid her off his lap, stood, then picked her up in his arms like he was carrying her over the threshold again. "Poor thing…ya poor, poor darlin'. My God, I cain't imagine what that musta been like." Then her rested his forehead against hers and softly began to weep with her.

Lily couldn't react to it, it was so unexpected. She could only cry in his big, strong arms as he paced back and forth, his head still resting on hers, his arms holding her tight against him like she was a child being comforted after a nightmare. Several times he stopped and looked at the sky, his mouth moving without sound, and she realized he was praying. If she didn't know any better, she'd say he was thanking God that she was alive.

She didn't know what to do now. It was one thing for someone to hear her story, another to see the results—and even now, he'd only gotten a tiny glimpse, not the whole picture. Would he be repulsed by her anyway? Would he want to be around her after seeing what she'd suffered? No one ever had before.

When they both ran out of tears for the moment, Oscar set her on her feet. "Lily, honey, I'm so sorry 'bout what happened to ya, and yer mother-in-law. No one should hafta suffer like ya did. Out here, the war didn't touch us much—all we knew was what folks told us when they passed through. And back then, this wasn't even a real stage stop. We just let folks rest a couple days 'fore they moved on. We kinda escaped all the worst of it."

She wrapped her arms around him and held on tight. "I'm glad you did, for your sake. This place is like a refuge, a safe haven. I love it here. I know that sounds silly, as I only arrived yesterday. But I already love it."

"That don't surprise me none, honey. Everyone loves this place. That's why some folks come just to come—they like the food and the company, and that's all right by us."

Lily sniffled, wiped her eyes and looked up at him. "You won't think I'm ugly?"

Oscar smiled warmly and shook his head. "How could I ever think that, Lily Fair? You're my wife— 'for better or worse, for richer or poorer.' 'Sides, I don't exactly look like Harrison or Colin Cooke— them are some handsome men, any woman'll tell ya. And ya should've seen their older brother, Duncan. 'Member I told ya about him and how he ended up movin' to England?"

"Yes, I remember. But I…" She found herself laughing. "… I didn't believe a word of it…"

"Hey, I told ya true. The man's an honest-to-God duke. But that's not the point. I know I'm nothing special as looks go. I know what folks say about me—the stuff they say to my face, and what they tell Ma and my brothers when they think I won't find out. And it don't matter one bitty bit."

"What do they say? Are you going to tell me?"

He brushed a lock of hair out of her eyes, bent down and kissed her on the forehead. "Are ya gonna show me?"

Lily's first reaction was to pull away, but she didn't. He had a right to see. He was going to see them anyway—why not now? She wiped her eyes once more and took a deep breath. "You're sure no one's around?"

"I'm sure. Anson and Henry got chores to do and Ma's probably sewing about now. Besides, they all know I brought ya down here to steal a kiss or two from ya."

Lily gasped in shock. "Oscar White, I declare!"

He chuckled, a deep rumble Lily swore she could feel in her chest.

She stood, stepped away and glanced around, just in case, took another deep breath, then began undoing the buttons of her dress. With gritted teeth and eyes closed tight she lifted it over her head, then did the same with her shift. Finally, suppressing a whimper of terror, she pulled her underthings down and stepped out of them before opening her eyes again. "There. This is me, Oscar. I wish I could give you better, but…"

Oscar didn't say a word, just stared for a full minute. Then he slowly got up and walked around her, a silent inspection. She felt like an ancient statue in a museum—one that had been badly damaged and pieced back together haphazardly. Time went by, two minutes, three. And still he remained silent.

Lily had no idea what he was thinking. The only people who'd seen her in this state since the fire were women. And all of them were so repulsed by the sight that they'd given her the first excuse they could think of and left as fast as their legs could carry them. No man had ever seen her scars except the doctors that treated her burns, most of whom had told her she would die (and a few who'd said it would be a mercy). But she'd fought hard for her life.

Now here she was, naked as the day she was born, praying her husband wouldn't be revolted by her hideous body…

"Lily Fair?"

She opened her eyes, not realizing she'd closed them again.

Oscar stood in front of her, tears running unchecked down his face. His voice was hoarse, thick with emotion. "Lily Fair, you are the most beautiful thing I've ever seen."

"But, Osc—" Her objection was cut off by his lips on hers, his arms around her back. She gave in, grabbing his belt—her upper arms pinned by his— and pulling herself closer.

When he finally pulled away an eternity or two later, he looked into her eyes in wonder. "And I ain't just sayin' yer beautiful out here, though ya are." He tapped her shoulder. "I mean here too." He put a hand over her heart. "And here." He moved his hand to her head. "I cain't fathom what that was like for ya, but ya beat it. Ya beat it and ya survived, and oh my, what a woman you are, Lily Fair. What a rare and beautiful woman."

"You really think I'm beautiful?"

"Yes, I do, Lily Fair. Every inch of ya, inside and out."

She still had trouble believing it. Didn't he see…? Or maybe…maybe it was she who didn't see. "You don't regret marrying me?"

Oscar's brow furrowed. "'Course not! What kinda silly question is that?"

"I thought it was a logical one," she said, running a finger down a scar on her sternum.

Hands on his hips, Oscar shook his head. "Woman, I can see you and I are gonna go a round or two over this. But I ain't gonna quarrel with ya today. Sure, ya got some bad scars on ya, and some men might be put off by that, but I ain't them."

Lily looked at him, her eyes filling with admiration. "I should say not."

He nodded. "Good. Now we got that settled, I have another place I wanna show you." He scooped her clothes off the ground and handed them to her.

"But…you mean…that's it?"

Oscar's eyebrow shot skyward. "Were ya hopin' for more? Ya *want* rejection? 'Cause if ya do, ya ain't gonna get it from me, Mrs. White. Now c'mon." Not waiting for her to dress, he took her by the hand and led her from the grassy banks of the pool.

"Where are we going?" she asked, feeling the need to say something, not to mention put her clothes on.

"You'll see. It's another special place."

Lily let him lead her up the trail along the creek for about ten minutes before it veered off into the woods and down a hill. There she slipped her shift over her head. After another ten minutes they reached the bottom of a small canyon. "What's that noise?" she asked, her ears picking up a faint roar.

"Ya'll see." Oscar squeezed her hand and continued on the trail. The ground was flat here, the canyon narrow, its upward slope on either side of them steeper the farther they walked.

The roar got louder, and soon she recognized the sound and gasped in delight. "It's a waterfall, isn't it?"

"Yep, and a right purty one too. Just like you are."

"I look like a waterfall?" she teased. The fact Oscar wasn't repulsed by her scars was still sinking in. She felt better, more confident her new husband wouldn't toss her aside and find himself a new wife. She'd underestimated him, a mistake on her part—she shouldn't have assumed the worst, but all she'd been through had caused her ability to look at the positive side of things to atrophy. Now it was waking up, and she liked the feeling.

"No, silly woman, ya ain't a waterfall," Oscar said. "'Less'n yer crying, but I do a fair share of that myself."

They'd stopped and she took a moment to look into his eyes. "It didn't bother me that you cried. In fact, it…made me feel better."

"Did it, now? Why d'ya suppose that is, Lily Fair?"

"Because you weren't weeping out of pity for me. You were weeping *with* me. There's a big difference, you know."

"Yeah, I know." He gave her hand another squeeze and led her on.

They went around a sharp bend, and there was the waterfall. It was only about fifteen feet high, but it was wide and loud and filled the air with misty spray. Lily saw the rainbow it made and smiled in delight. "Oh, Oscar, this is beautiful."

"Ain't it, though? I love comin' here."

"Do you do your thinking here too?"

"Nah, but I do like standin' under the waterfall when it's real hot. That water sure does cool ya off." He put an arm around her and kissed the top of her head.

She smiled and leaned against him, enjoying the warmth against her partially still-bare skin. Funny, she hadn't noticed she'd walked that whole way with him with hardly a stitch on. But she felt so safe with him, so accepted, that she hadn't felt the need to cover completely up. "What was it like living here all your life?" she asked. "Never going anywhere, seeing only the people passing through?"

"Well, it ain't like we never leave. But I like living in a place so beautiful, I don't have to seek beauty anywhere else." He faced her and looked into her eyes. "You were the only beauty that was missin'."

Lily's lower lip trembled and the tears started again. But for once, they were tears of joy. She dropped the rest of her clothes on the ground and pulled Oscar close.

Eventually she and Oscar got dressed and headed back to the house. Where the trail was wide enough he'd put an arm around her and she'd rest her head on his shoulder. His legs being so much longer than hers made it a little clumsy, but Oscar did his best to match her pace. They didn't talk much, just enjoyed each other's quiet company.

She noticed Oscar always held her hand or was touching her somehow, a silent reminder that he wasn't going anywhere and wasn't going to send her away either. He'd accepted her, scars and all—and then some. She realized how blessed she was and almost cried several times along the trail, but managed to keep the tears at bay.

When they got home Ma was already busy preparing lunch. "I was wonnerin' when y'two were comin' back. How was the creek?"

Lily smiled. "I thought it was wonderful."

Oscar grinned. "So did I. It's even better with Lily there."

"Glad t'hear it," Ma said, her eyebrow raised. Lily got the impression the woman knew they'd done more than just look at a body of water, but she didn't mind. Mothers always knew. "Now yer back,

Oscar, ya wanna help yer brothers fer a minute in th'barn, while I have Lily help me?"

"Sure, Ma." Oscar said. "What're they havin' trouble with?"

"Tryna figger out where t'put yer weddin' present."

"Oh, that," he said with a laugh. "I plumb forgot."

Lily nodded, having forgotten too, then remembered the Cookes' gift. "The cattle and bulls…will they need a lot of room?"

"Depends on how much they like to wander," Oscar said. "The Triple-C Ranch has plenty of grazin' land. We got some pasture beyond the trees behind the barn, but I'm sure we'll hafta fence off more."

"Oh dear," Lily said. "I won't be much help with that."

"'Course y'won't," Ma said. "Ya'll be helpin' me in here while th'men figger 'at out."

Oscar went to the sideboard where he always kept a full water pitcher and poured himself and Lily a glass. He handed her one, then drained his. He'd mentioned he kept the water handy, as cooking was hot work. "Don't worry, Ma, we'll come up with somethin'." He set down his glass and looked at Lily. "You gonna be all right, honey?"

Her stomach fluttered at the endearment, even though he'd been calling her that all day. "Oh, I'm quite all right now…" She blushed, realizing that she meant more than just his acceptance of her scars. The time they'd spent by the waterfall…

He smiled back, knowing what she meant, and went out the back door.

Ma was chuckling. "My my, y'two did have a good walk, din'tcha?" She winked with her good eye.

Lily smiled despite her embarrassment. She had, but for more reasons than just what her mother-in-law was thinking. "Indeed."

Chapter Twelve

After lunch preparation, Lily sat down with Ma for a lesson in mending. "Ya never mended 'fore?" Ma asked in surprise.

"Only a little, when I lived with my aunt in Denver. I…" Oh heavens, she couldn't tell the woman she'd thought she was above performing such a menial task. "…wasn't very good." That was a version of the truth. Really, she hadn't been a very good *person*—uncharitable, unhelpful, unproductive.

After seeing Oscar's reaction to her terrible secret, she was beginning to realize just how petty she'd been. Toward the end of her aunt's life it was getting to the point where the two women were happy for scraps, but it wouldn't have gotten that far if Lily'd had a mind to work. The least she could've done was her aunt's mending on a regular basis. But no, she'd let the poor woman struggle with that until her dying day.

"I'll show ya some simple stitches 'n give ya the easy stuff t'start," Ma told her.

"Thank you, I appreciate that. I'm afraid I have a lot to learn."

"Don't worry none, chile, we'll teach ya everythin' ya need to know. I'm juss glad yer here. In time, them helpin' hands o'yers'll learn a lot."

Lily giggled at her words. "Was it hard for you to manage while Oscar went to get me?"

"A li'l. Henry picked up the place 'n did the laundry 'n dishwashin'. I cooked, 'n Anson saw to the stock 'n outside. But 'round here y'sure notice when there's a body missin'. Havin' an extra one's a blessin'."

"I hope I'm able to bless you sooner rather than later."

"Ain't you doin' the blessin', chile—that'd be th'good Lord. Dunno what His plans are most times, but we're happy He sent ya here."

Lily smiled in amazement. In her eyes, *she* was the one being blessed, not her new family. Oscar had done in a few hours that morning what years of praying hadn't—he'd made her feel good about herself, accepted her. Or was that the Lord telling her how *He* felt through her new husband, as if Oscar was the Almighty's hands extended? "My goodness," she whispered.

"Whassat, chile?" Ma asked.

"Oh, nothing, just thinking aloud." Lily hoped Ma had a handkerchief handy—she suddenly felt like crying again. The good Lord *had* answered her prayers, through Oscar! And it wasn't only Oscar He'd blessed her with, but a whole new family. She buried her face in her hands and shook with silent sobs.

Ma put a hand on her shaking shoulder. "Why, whass the matter, chile?"

Lily lifted her face, wet with tears. "I'm sorry, it's just that this day has been so wonderful. I can't tell you how much."

Ma smiled at her. "Well, 'at's how the Lord tends t'work, bringin' all stuff t'gether fer His good purpose."

Lily nodded and wiped her tears away with her hand. "All right, I think I have a hold of myself."

Ma laughed. "Chile, when it comes t'the Lord 'n His business, ya never have a hold o' yerself. Best 'member that."

Lily laughed and they got to mending.

The lesson was short, easy and soon she'd stitched up a pair of worn socks. "Socks're the worst," Ma explained. "'Specially Henry's. Once yer ready, ya can tend Oscar's stuff 'n I'll take care of the others'. Juss be glad Oscar ain't as hard on his clothes as Henry."

Thank Heaven for that, Lily thought. It probably had to do with Oscar working more in the kitchen than outside. And speaking of the kitchen... "What is Oscar's favorite dessert?" Mending his things, she felt a growing urge to do something nice for him, but all her skills fell woefully short. Except maybe baking—therein lay her hope.

"Well, lemme think," Ma said. "I gotta choc'late cake recipe he likes—a guest gave it t'me some years back, said't came all the way from Paris, France. Oscar ain't never 'sperimented with that one—guess he figgers best not t'mess with perfection."

Lily laughed and clapped her hands. "My heavens, is it that good?"

"Yep, but it's hard to get choc'late out here. I can show y'the recipe 'n we'll see if we got everythin', but I'll prob'ly have to have Willie get some stuff from the Dunnigans. 'N if they don't have none, Sally Upton will—fer a price."

"That's one good thing about all the stagecoaches coming through here, isn't it? At least they can pick up supplies for you now and then. It's also a good thing the people in Clear Creek are so friendly…" That gave Lily another idea. "Ma, does Oscar like to read?"

"Oh yeah, in th'evenins when he has a spare moment. Depends on how full up we are 'n how much work there is."

"Does he have any books here he hasn't read yet?"

"Nah, he's read 'em all. Sev'ral times, most o'em."

"Does he ever think to get new books?"

"Nah, not when we need the money fer other stuff."

"I see," Lily said, her eyes downcast. With no

money of her own, how could she buy a book for her husband?

"Whass the matter, chile?"

"I just thought it would be nice to buy Oscar a new book, but I haven't any money."

"Don't mean ya cain't earn some."

"Earn? But how? Surely you're not thinking of paying me."

"Heaven's sake, chile, no. We're all in this t'gether. But it don't mean ya cain't make sumpin' t'sell the folks comin' through here."

Lily's eyes lit up. She hadn't thought of that. "Like what?"

Ma smiled slyly on her good side. "'Member 'at pie th'Truitts were hankerin' after? And ya offered t'give 'em one?"

"Yes, but what about…oh." Lily's eyes widened. "You mean sell them one?"

"Well, not *them*—ya already told 'em theirs was a gift. But if ya can bake stuff fer folks t'take on the road, maybe ya got somethin'. We never done it only 'cause it's more work 'n we ain't had th'time. But now yer here…"

Lily's face broke into a smile, and she hugged her new mother-in-law. "That's a wonderful idea!" Her expression suddenly went flat. "But I don't know if I bake *that* well."

Ma laughed. "Don't worry, chile. If ya don't now, ya will once we're through with ya!"

Three days later...

"Thass right, now don't overmix it," Ma advised as she watched Lily stir a bowl of cake batter.

"I'm so excited," Lily said. "I thought I knew how to do this, but this is far beyond anything I tried on my own."

"Cookin's an art t'some folks. I know 'tis t'my Oscar. He'll be a happy man when he finds out 'is wife can cook 'n bake 'longside'im. Not o'ernight, mind, but ya'll get there."

"I can hardly wait. I've done so little with my life before now. I feel like I've wasted it."

Ma put a hand on Lily's to stop her rapid stirring. "Not so fass. 'N I don't mean th'batter. Well... I do mean th'batter—time t'pour't into th'pans. But I also mean yer life. Don't be so quick t'think it was a waste, chile."

Lily started pouring and gave that some thought. Ma didn't know how she'd squandered all those years by being spoiled, demanding and ignorant of the hardships of others. Until the war came, and even then, she wasn't of much use.

"Look at me, chile."

Lily did, seeing the disfigured face of the woman before her. Ma had seen hard times too.

"Yer here, ain't ya? Y'ain't wastin' yer life now."

"No, but what about before..."

Ma held up a hand to silence her. "Lemme tell ya somethin', chile. Th'Lord don't waste nothin'.

Y'might think He does, 'cause y'cain't see what He's doin'. But there's plenty o' other folks who feel like ya do. Sometimes I have, I don't mind sayin', and don't think we ain't heard tales from ever'one else's come through here."

Lily blinked a few times, her mouth half open in shock. She hadn't thought about that before—why else would most people head west to start over? "I'm sorry, Ma. I didn't mean to imply that no one else suffered."

"Didn't think ya did. But ya were *implyin'* yer life was a waste. It weren't—it was *preparation*."

Lily finished pouring and set the bowl on the worktable. "But…before coming here I did nothing that wasn't selfish or petty or…well, I wasn't a good person. In fact, I was a snob. I thought myself better than everyone else."

Ma laughed. "You 'n ten thousan' others like ya. Plenty o' spoiled girls out there ain't gotta clue 'bout how life really works. But ya ain't that no more, are ya? Ya grown up some, right? 'Cause ya seem purty decent to me now."

"Only because I was forced to become decent."

"Seems t'me th'decency was already in there. Juss needed a li'l proddin' t'come out."

Tears stung the back of Lily's eyes. "Why are you being so kind to me?"

Ma surprised her, pulling her into her arms. "Dear chile, I been prayin' fer years fer th'Lord to bring Oscar a wife. I din't ask fer perfection. I asked Him to bring my son th'woman he needed most, 'n needed him most. 'N look who He sent."

Lily's lower lip began trembling. "How did you get so wise?"

Ma smiled. "Th'hard way. 'S the only way anyone does." She let Lily go and turned to the worktable. "Now let's get these pans in th'oven."

Lily contemplated Ma's words as the cakes baked and she helped Ma start supper. Oscar, Henry and Anson had all been busy the last several days cutting down trees and making fence posts in preparation for the cattle's arrival. It was hard work, and Lily did her best to help Ma with all the chores so the men wouldn't have to. "I'd best take the laundry off the line," she said, wiping her hands on her apron.

"You do that and I'll see to my dough," Ma replied. She was making her famous chicken and dumplings for supper, and Lily couldn't wait to see if they were as good as Sally Upton's.

Lily looked at the pot simmering on the stove. She'd watched Ma prepare the chicken in fascination, not sure if she'd ever have enough nerve to kill one of the birds and do everything else that had to be done to prepare it for cooking. But eventually, she knew, she'd have to learn.

She went out the kitchen's back door, picked up the large basket she'd left next to it and looked at the bedsheets billowing in the breeze. Spring was just now filling the air with the sweet smell of the first wildflowers.

As she took sheets off the line and put them in the basket, she thought of the last few nights and how tender and gentle Oscar had been. He'd held her, kissed her, made her feel things she had felt only briefly before with John, and so much more. She loved his deep gentle voice, large hands and lumbering ways. And his patience—so much patience, almost as if he was courting her. Of course, they'd gone well past courting that morning by the waterfall, but he still treated her as gentlemanly as he could.

She removed the last sheet, put it in the basket and turned back to the house. Even after consummating their marriage, Oscar was giving her time to feel comfortable with him. And she was, more and more. He touched her with loving adoration—no wincing or pulling his hands away from her scars, no grunts of disgust. And all the while, he told her how beautiful she was.

Lily bowed her head and closed her eyes. *Oh Lord, I don't deserve him. But thank You, thank You for giving me this man. I never could have found him on my own. I know I couldn't. Thank You.*

She opened her eyes, took a deep breath and carried the laundry into the house. Once it was all folded—the easiest chore in the world; it had taken her all of a half-hour to learn—she returned to the kitchen to help Ma with supper. She set the table and watched in fascination as Ma made her dumplings.

Not long after, Oscar, Henry and Anson came in

to eat. "Somethin' smells good," Oscar commented. "Need any help, Lily Fair?"

"Thank you, but no. Go wash up."

"Well, look at you, Mrs. White—married to me less than two weeks and already bossin' me 'round."

"Your ma's been teaching me well. I'm sure I'll get bossier as time goes on." She grinned and waved a spoon at him.

He laughed and headed out to the pump.

There were no guests tonight, just family, and Lily discovered she liked these evenings the best. Not that the stagecoach passengers weren't interesting, but she enjoyed the closeness of just the five of them after all those years alone or nearly so.

She sighed with satisfaction and thought of her cake, already frosted and resting on top of the hutch in the kitchen. Ma had warned her Henry was in the habit of running a finger through the frosting if it was within reach, no matter how many times she or Oscar told him not to. He just couldn't help himself. She wondered if Henry would ever marry.

Anson would, she was sure. He already had set his sights on a young woman in Clear Creek named Emeline Turner, and she'd helped him pen a letter to her last night. Willie would take it to Clear Creek when he came through tomorrow. Would Anson be crushed if she didn't answer? And if she did answer, what then? How could they court when they lived so far apart, other than by mail?

"Is supper ready?" Lily asked Ma as she re-entered the kitchen.

Ma was ladling the main course into a tureen. "Sure is. Carry this t'th'table, will ya? Careful, it's hot."

Grabbing two dishrags, Lily carefully picked up the chicken and dumplings and carried it to the table, then went back for the sliced bread and a big bowl of vegetables. None of the men were in the kitchen at the moment, so Lily glanced at the top of the hutch. "Have any of them seen it yet?"

Ma smiled. "Not yet, thank Heaven, or there'd be a long mark on it from Henry's finger. Ya know, thass why I usually stick with pies?"

Lily laughed. She was looking forward to surprising Oscar. For the first time in a very long time, she felt at peace.

Chapter Thirteen

Three weeks later...

"Ma!" Henry yelled from the porch. "Stage's comin'!"

Lily and Ma hurried to finish setting the table as Henry came through the screen door Oscar had installed just that morning. It was warm for early May in Oregon, but Lily and the rest of the family hoped it stayed that way for a few days. Last week it had rained like Noah's flood, and they were hoping to dry out.

"Think we'll be full up?" Henry asked.

"Now, Henry," Ma said. "Ya know's well as I do we won't know 'til it gets here. Ya bring my wood in yet?"

"Did Lily bake another cake?"

"Thass none o' yer business 'til it's time fer dessert. Now, my wood?"

Henry grinned cockily. "I brought it in a few minutes ago, Ma. Ya been in here a while."

"Thass 'cause o'th'extra work from havin' so many folks here last night. I cain't 'member bein' so busy."

"Good thing yer here now, Lily," Henry said in all seriousness. "It sure helps Ma out, and makes her happy. Makes me happy too—'specially when ya bake a cake."

Lily was still adjusting to Henry's ways. "Thank you, I'm glad to be here. And Henry?"

"Yeah?"

"Yes, I made a cake tonight. But keep your fingers out of it or you won't get any."

Henry stared at his shoes. "Yes, ma'am."

Lily laughed and gave him a quick peck on the cheek as the stage pulled up in front of the house. "Well," she said, "here we go." By now she was used to the routine. Most of the time, Ma kept her busy in the kitchen and with other household chores, staying ready for the stage passengers. This freed Oscar to help his brothers build the corral for the cattle coming soon. The Cookes had sent word via Willie the last time he came through that their wedding present was already on its way.

Unfortunately, Anson had been hoping for another message, one that hadn't yet come. So far there was no letter from Emeline Turner. He understood he needed to be patient, but he couldn't hide his disappointment.

"I hope Willie's got sumpin' fer Anson t'day," Ma said as if reading Lily's thoughts. "That boy o' mine's been prancing 'round the last week like a nervous horse."

"He's not the only one waiting," Lily added. "I still haven't heard back from Belle or Sadie."

"And I'm wonderin' what's for supper," Oscar boomed behind them.

Both women jumped. "Land sakes, Oscar!" Ma cried. "Don't do that!"

Oscar put an arm around each of them and gave them a hug. "Just playin' with ya, Ma," he said with a laugh.

Before either of them could respond, Willie opened the screen door for the first of the passengers. "Welcome to the Whites' Stage Stop, Mrs. Cooke."

Lily turned to look, then barreled around the table. "Sadie! What are you doing here?"

"I thought I'd surprise you with a little visit. I'm afraid Belle couldn't come—she has too many children to look after. Thankfully my eldest Honoria is taking my place while I'm gone."

Lily couldn't stop grinning. "Oh my goodness, this is wonderful! I'm sorry Belle couldn't come, but...*this* is wonderful!"

Sadie laughed and turned to Ma. "Mrs. White, I'll thank you now for your hospitality, but don't be afraid to put me to work."

"Believe me, chile, I won't be 'fraid," Ma laughed.

"Did ya know she was comin'?" Oscar asked his mother with a smile.

"'Course I did—Willie brought me a note last time he was here, 'n I thought I'd let't be a s'prise."

Oscar laughed and shook his head. "Well, it sure is!"

The passengers filed in—a young couple with a baby, and a woman that looked about Lily's age. They all did what passengers usually did the moment they walked through the door—namely, stared at Ma. But she took it in stride. "Welcome, folks!" she slurred as she hustled out to the counter and opened the guestbook. "I'm Mrs. White. Ya can sign in here, 'n Lily'll show ya t'yer rooms. Ya got anythin' heavy we need t'bring up?"

The young couple shook their heads. "N-n-n-no, ma'am," the gentleman said.

"'N you are?"

"Mr. and Mrs. Samuel B-Beecher, ma'am."

They couldn't be more than twenty, Lily thought, their baby perhaps a year old. The young mother, a petite blonde, shifted the child from hip to hip as it squirmed in her arms. They both looked haggard. "Here, let me take your satchels for you," Lily said, feeling the urge to relieve the poor souls from at least some of their burdens.

"Thank you," the mother said in relief.

"My pleasure." She picked up both their satchels, wondering if the poor pair would fall asleep in their room and miss supper. She led them up the stairs to the second room on the right, explaining, "We have a cradle in here. I'm sure your little one will be comfortable in it."

"If he ever stops moving," Mrs. Beecher groaned. "He's like this all the time. That long stage ride didn't help."

Lily opened the door and let them in. "I'm sure after he's had a chance to play and rest, he'll be fine." Then again, what did she know—the child might cry all night. Wouldn't that be a treat?

She tried not to dwell on the thought that she was no expert on motherhood—she'd never raised children. Maybe Sadie could enlighten her—she had four of her own. Ma had told her a few things concerning children, but her boys were grown men now. Sadie (and Belle) had more recent experience, as most of theirs were still young.

"Supper will be served in an hour," Lily told them. "If you'll excuse me, I have to show the other passengers to their rooms."

Mr. Beecher nodded his thanks before turning back to his family. Lily slipped out, closed the door and hurried downstairs to find Sadie chatting with the other passenger, who now had a large trunk next to her. "Oh dear," Lily muttered. "I think I'm going to need Henry's help with that."

"Oh, there's no need," the woman insisted. Her accent was flat, Midwestern, with just a touch of New England bray. "I can just remove what I need for the night."

"Nonsense," Lily assured her. "Henry won't mind

carrying it up to your room and bringing it down in the morning. It'll be fine."

"Well, as long as it's no trouble…"

"She's right, Henry won't mind," Sadie said, then turned to Lily. "This is Miss Evangeline Norton. She's a schoolteacher."

"Oh?" Lily said with interest. "Are you going to Oregon City to visit family or to work?"

"Actually, I'm not going that far. I'm traveling to The Dalles to take up a teaching position there."

"The Dalles?" Lily said, then looked at Sadie.

"It's a town up on the Columbia River between here and Portland," Sadie explained. "I've heard of it, but I've never been there myself."

"Oh, I see," Lily said. "Welcome to Oregon, Miss Norton. I only recently came to Oregon from Denver."

Miss Norton smiled stiffly. "I'm from Cleveland, Ohio, originally. By your accent, I gather you came to Denver from the South?"

"Charleston, South Carolina," Lily confirmed, noticing her unease. The War Between the States might have ended a decade before, but it remained fresh in people's memories. Lily hoped Miss Norton hadn't lost too much in the war, but from the look on her face, she'd obviously lost a few. Now here she was, being greeted by a Texan and a Carolinian…well, at least she was being a lady about it. "I'd best get Henry," Lily continued, hoping to ease the tension.

It seemed to work. "I…I'm terribly sorry," Miss Norton stammered. "I didn't mean to stare."

"Think nothing of it," Lily said. She had to remain hospitable, after all, but she did wonder. Well, she'd make sure not to bring up the war—that would only cause trouble. She went into the kitchen and found Henry munching on a cookie. "Henry, I need your help. And stay out of those—you'll spoil your supper."

Henry chuckled, stuffed the rest of the cookie into his mouth and followed Lily into the front room. "What do ya need, Lily?"

"Can you take Miss Norton's trunk up to her room and…" Lily stopped. Henry was staring at Miss Norton much the same way she'd been staring at Lily earlier. "Oh no." Ma and Oscar had both warned her how easily Henry became infatuated with some of the women passengers, but had also said he wasn't nearly as bad as he used to be. If that was the case, what was she to do about the puppy-dog look he was giving her?

Then she saw Miss Norton had a look on her face like she was trying to decide whether or not to take home the puppy! "Er… Henry? Miss Norton's trunk?"

Henry jumped at her voice. "Oh yeah. Sorry, Lily." He bent down, hefted the trunk onto one shoulder and straightened. "Which room?"

"Number four." Lily turned to Miss Norton. "Follow me, please."

Miss Norton took a last look at Henry then hurried after Lily. "My, but he's strong, isn't he?"

"Yes, he is. Almost as strong as my husband, Oscar, Henry's older brother."

"I see. What a fine young man." Miss Norton glanced over her shoulder and gave Henry a smile. He smiled back as he ascended the stairs, almost lost his balance, but righted himself and grinned. Miss Norton laughed. "Well done, sir. But please be careful."

"Don't ya worry, ma'am. I will!" Henry trotted up the remaining stairs and sauntered down the hall and into Miss Norton's room, passing the women as he did. "Where would ya like it, ma'am?"

"Anywhere in the room is fine, thank you," Miss Norton said. She sounded impressed. Oh dear— Henry would be beside himself for the rest of the evening, and likely beside Miss Norton if given half a chance. Lily hoped he remembered she was leaving in the morning.

Lily took a moment to study the schoolteacher as she, in turn, studied Henry. Miss Norton had light brown hair, blue eyes and an average build, a little thick around the middle. That made sense—she was clearly over thirty, and how much physical work was there to teaching children anyway? "Supper is in an hour," she told her. "If you need anything in the meantime, just come downstairs and ask."

"Ya can ask me too," Henry gushed.

"Thank you, I'll be sure to ask one of you should I need anything," Miss Norton replied, smiling at Henry.

Lily nonchalantly covered her mouth with her hand as Henry continued grinning. And not moving. "Henry? We should go now."

"Oh, uh, yeah…" He finally started moving his feet, though his eyes stayed fixed on Miss Norton.

Lily shook her head. This was not going to end well if he didn't get whatever ideas he had in his head out of it. "Remember what I told you earlier about the cake?"

Henry's head moved in her direction, but still not his eyes. "Uh-huh."

Lily sighed and took Henry by the hand. She would have to tell Oscar about this, before it got worse. "Come on, we have chores to do."

"Uh-huh," Henry said, letting Lily drag him out while still smiling back at the teacher.

As soon as she closed the door behind them, Lily spun on her brother-in-law. "Henry, what has gotten into you?" she admonished quietly. "You know it's rude to stare."

"Well…yeah, I know that."

"Then why were you ogling Miss Norton like that?"

"But she stared at me first! Ain't rude when they stare at ya first."

Lily put her hands on her hips. "Who told you that?"

"Uh… I dunno. I just figgered…"

Lily was having a hard time staying angry—actually, she was having a hard time not laughing. Henry did have his own brand of logic. Finally she grinned and kissed him on the cheek. "Henry, I love you, you silly duck."

Henry beamed. "Aw gee, Lily, thanks for sayin' so. But don't say it too loud, or Oscar'll be jealous on account ya said ya loved me. I ain't heard ya say that to him."

Lily frowned. Merciful heavens, Henry was probably right! She liked him, certainly, even though they'd only been married a little over a month. But had she ever actually said so?

Was she really in love with him? Or did she just appreciate what he'd done for her? Now that Henry had brought it up, she'd have to examine how she felt. She'd fallen into the family's busy routine over the last few weeks, and it hadn't left much time to pay attention to her feelings. Did she *love* him?

"What's the matter, Lily?" Henry asked.

Lily jumped. "Oh goodness…"

Henry laughed. "Sorry to startle ya. But I thought ya said we had chores?"

She quickly nodded and rubbed her temples. "Yes, we do. I have to help Oscar with the rolls, and I think he wanted you to help Willie."

"I'll ask him. C'mon, let's not be flappin' our gums on the stairs, or Ma'll tan our hides."

She smiled. "Aren't we a little old for that?"

"She don't think I am, or she wouldn't threaten to do it."

Lily laughed. "Oh, Henry, you really are special." She wrapped her arm through his, and together they went downstairs.

Chapter Fourteen

Supper was an interesting affair, with Miss Norton and Henry stealing glances at one another all the while. At least they weren't outright gawking at each other anymore. But Willie and Abe noticed, and the two drivers did their best to keep their chuckles in check. Meanwhile, Abe's one passenger, a tall, gruff-looking, middle-aged fellow, only said two words— "thank you"—the entire meal. Lily hadn't caught his name, but at least he had good manners.

Anson was the one out of character—slouched in his chair, picking at his food. There was still no return letter from Emeline Turner, and his disappointment was so obvious it even caught Abe's attention. "What's the matter with you? You look like you just had to shoot your horse."

Anson straightened in his chair. "Nothing." He poked a chunk of potato with his fork and popped it in his mouth.

Abe squinted his right eye at him. "This have anything to do with…"

"Don't," Oscar said, his deep voice stern.

Abe leaned back and brought both hands up. "Just asking. Didn't mean any harm."

"I know," Oscar said. "But Anson's doin' 'nough harm all by himself. He don't need an excuse to do more."

Lily cringed. Oscar had just informed everyone Anson was feeling sorry for himself, and Anson looked ready to explode. Never mind that it was true—unrequited love was painful, and bringing it up didn't make it better. She wondered if Oscar felt the same—she was still pondering Henry's quip upstairs. Did she love him? For that matter, did he love her? One fling at the waterfall—albeit replicated a few times in their own room—wasn't entirely an answer.

She watched her husband out the corner of her eye as he spooned himself another serving of fried potatoes, then turned to her. "Would you like some more?"

She smiled shyly. "No, thank you." If he knew what she'd been thinking about, would he feel the same?

But to Lily, the words, "I love you," were not to be taken lightly. She wanted to make sure she was absolutely sure before she uttered them. She certainly hoped he felt the same. He *acted* like he did, but he hadn't spoken them either. At least he wasn't repulsed by her—that counted for a lot—and they had consummated their marriage. But doubts remained.

She looked at Oscar as he continued to eat—he was still busy watching Anson—then surveyed the rest of the table, the people and the large inviting room that housed them. This was her home now, her family, her life. And she liked it. She sighed in contentment as peace permeated the very marrow of her bones. She belonged here, she realized. And, more importantly, she belonged with Oscar.

Lily studied him again, a tiny smile on her lips, and knew. Yes, she *was* in love with her husband. Which meant the next step was to say so…and hope he did the same.

Everything was quiet after breakfast the next day—too quiet, Lily thought. Anson was still moping, but that was to be expected. The greater problem was Henry, standing on the front porch and staring forlornly down the lane to the main road. She and Ma were in the living room, watching him through the front window. "Is he going to be all right?" she asked Ma.

Ma shook her head. "Gotta admit, he ain't never done this 'fore."

"Stare like that, you mean?"

"Oh, th'boy stares, no doubt, but he stares at what's in front o'im. That schoolmarm's gone, 'n he's starin' where she usta be."

Henry walked to the end of the porch and sat on the railing, eyes still intent on the path.

"He's got th'real thing this time, I'm 'fraid," Ma said in dismay. "'N I ain't sure what t'do 'bout it."

"You mean, he's in love?" Lily said, her voice cracking. "But he just met the woman!"

"Sometimes 'at's all it takes."

"But how... I... No, he couldn't possibly be."

Ma glared at her. "Chile, y'gotta lot t'learn 'bout love. 'N Henry ain't like the rest o' us." She turned back to the window. "Sometimes I envy him. When he makes up 'is mind, he sticks t'it."

"But...doesn't he realize she's not coming back?"

She nodded slowly. "Th'knowin' part o' him does, but th'hopin' part o'im's still hangin' on t'th'chance she might."

Lily's sigh was heartfelt. "Poor Henry."

"Poor Henry? Poor us—he's likely t'sit there starin' at th'road all day. 'N then who does his chores?" Ma shook her head again. "Hope he ain't so bad he stops eatin'."

Lily's mouth fell open. "Are you serious?"

"Aw yeah. If he made up his mind 'bout her, he won't think o' nothin' else."

Lily didn't know whether to laugh or cry at that. What woman wouldn't want a man with such single-minded devotion to her? It made her heart melt just thinking about it.

But all the White men had that quality. Anson had letters already penned to Emeline, ready to send, and she'd read some of them. He'd told Emeline about himself, what he did for the stage stop, how his days were spent, how beautiful it was there, that their table was never empty nor their larders spare. He was presenting himself as best he could on paper, without actually courting. But until she responded, he could do nothing. And if her eventual reply was "thank you, but no, thank you," he might end up staring off into the distance with Henry.

Did the younger men come by that naturally, or had they learned it from Oscar? He watched over Lily like a hen over her chicks, always present or close by, offering comfort and adoration. He told her how beautiful she was daily, and showed her nightly. For so long she'd thought of herself as a walking blemish, nothing pure or beautiful about her. But Oscar didn't see her that way.

Oscar told her he saw bravery in her scars, a courage lacking in most of the people he'd seen come through. He saw devotion, resilience, perseverance, a great compassion for others and an appreciation for life. And she was beginning to see it too, beginning to disperse the shadows that had obscured her vision for so long.

And she was dispelling her own selfishness and snobbery too. Years ago she'd have had nothing to do with someone like Henry, or the rest of the Whites for that matter. They were what her father would've called backwoods hill-dwelling hicks. What, she wondered, would he say now? "Oh, Daddy…" she whispered.

"What, chile?" Ma said.

"Nothing." Lily gazed out the window at Henry one last time, then turned toward the kitchen. She and Ma had chores to do. She just hoped Henry got around to doing his.

"Oscar?" Lily whispered in his ear.

"Mm?"

"I'm worried about your brothers."

Oscar opened one eye, then the other. "Don't be. They'll manage." He pulled her closer, enjoying the warmth of her body against his. Her soft cotton nightdress was new, a present he'd ordered when he sent Willie off with his list of supplies for the stage stop a few weeks ago. He'd given it to her after supper as a surprise, and she'd cried and hugged him so hard he'd lost his breath.

"Henry started making a chair for Miss Norton. Don't you think you should speak with him?"

"Won't do no good. Once Henry's got somethin' in his head, that's it. To him it's real. He's gotta figger out on his own that it ain't."

"How long will that take?" she asked.

Oscar shrugged, just enough so she'd feel it. "With Henry, ya never know. Though I suspect this time it might take a while. Ya don't wanna encourage him, but ya don't wanna discourage him neither."

"Very helpful," she teased.

"Helpful as I can be, honey. How're you and Sadie gettin' along?"

"I'm not sure—Ma has been running us both ragged, so we haven't been able to spend much time together yet. Poor Sadie will never want to visit me again."

"Tomorrow ya have time—it's a family day, re-member? No stages comin' through."

"Thank Heaven for that." She kissed him on the cheek, then snuggled closer.

Oscar sighed in contentment and relaxed. He should've gotten hitched years ago. But then, what guarantee was there that he'd have met Lily? No, the Almighty's timing was best. He was older and wiser now, and so was she. Now if they could just set a good example for his lovelorn brothers, all would be well in his world.

The next morning the family was up and about earlier than usual. Sadie helped Oscar and Lily pre-pare breakfast, then, along with Henry and Anson, surprised Ma with breakfast in bed. "Land sakes, ever'one!" she exclaimed when they burst into her bedroom. "Is it Christmas?"

"Nope," Oscar said. "We just happen to think we got the best momma in the world, and we wanted to let her know."

Ma wiped the tears from her eyes and smiled at the roomful of people. "Thank ya, thank ya so much. You three…make't four…" She looked at Lily. "…are the best kids a mother could have." She looked at Sadie.

"Ya'll know what I mean when yer younguns get a li'l older."

"I already do," Sadie said. "And not all of mine are so little anymore, remember? I still can't get over Honoria being sixteen."

"They grow fast, don't they?" Ma said as she looked at the food piled on her plate. "This looks wonnerful, whoever made't."

Oscar, Lily and Sadie smiled in return.

Henry stepped forward, reached in his pocket and pulled something out. "And I made this for ya, Ma." He handed her a small carved figure.

Ma took it, looked at it and gasped. "Why, Henry, this's lovely…" She held it up so everyone could see.

Oscar leaned forward. "Henry!"

"Henry," Anson said, eyes wide. "It's perfect."

Lily and Sadie exchanged a quick look. "What is it?" Lily asked.

Ma held it up a little higher. "It's th'spittin' image of my Josephus," she said, fresh tears in her eyes. "I ain't never seen nothin' so beautiful in my life. Thank ya, Henry—yer pa'd be so proud o' ya. This's somethin' all o' us can enjoy."

Henry blushed. "Aw shucks, Ma. I can make ones for Oscar and Anson too if they want."

"I want one," Anson said in a rush. "Can ya make mine bigger?"

"Sure. I made Ma's small 'cause I figgered she'd wanna carry Pa 'round in her pocket."

"Thass right consid'rate o' ya, Henry," Ma said. "How long ya younguns been cookin' this up?"

Oscar looked at Lily and Sadie. "We thought of it last night. Dunno how long Henry's been workin' on that, though."

"I was makin' it for yer birthday, Ma," Henry said. "But when Oscar said he was gonna surprise ya with breakfast in bed, I thought I'd give it to ya now."

Ma wiped at her eyes again. "Ya younguns're th'best thing ever happened t'me. I cain't stop sayin' it."

Sadie smiled. "You're a very blessed woman, Mrs. White, to have such sons, and now a daughter too. I hope my own children grow up to be as fine as them."

Lily straightened and Oscar caught the pride on her face. He reached over, took her hand and squeezed. She looked up at him and beamed. Life was good.

A loud, insistent rapping on the front door wasn't. "There ain't no stage comin' today," Henry said.

"Even if there was, they don't show up this early," Oscar commented. "Henry, stay with the women. Anson, come with me." He left their mother's room, Anson close on his heels, and went straight to the end of the hall where they kept two loaded shotguns for emergencies. He directed Anson to a window where he'd have a good view of most of the yard around the house, then headed to the front room.

By the time he got to the door, the pounding had stopped. "Who's there?" he shouted, not willing to open it just yet.

"Eli Turner!"

"Eli? Aw shoot, and here I was worried!" Oscar opened the door to find a disheveled, cut and bleeding Eli Turner leaning against the jamb. "What in tarnation happened to you?"

"Emeline…they got Emeline!" Eli took two steps toward him and collapsed.

"Jumpin' Jehoshaphat!" Oscar quickly picked Eli up like he was a rag doll and carried him to the sofa near the fireplace just as Anson—who must have heard the whole thing—came running into the room. "Anson, fetch some water, then get Ma. He needs doctorin'."

"But what 'bout Emeline?"

"We ain't gonna find out 'bout Emeline if we cain't bring Eli 'round. Now git!"

Anson spun, tripped, righted himself and ran outside to the pump. He was back in a minute with a cup of water, then raced upstairs, and soon everyone was gathered around Eli's limp form.

"What th'Sam Hill's goin' on?" Ma asked, then saw the cut on Eli's forehead and turned to Henry. "Get m'doctorin' bag."

"Right away, Ma!" Henry was off like a shot into the kitchen.

"He looks like he's been running through the woods," Sadie said as she examined him. "But what's he doing here?"

Henry returned with Ma's bag and set it on a small table near the sofa. Ma opened it and dug through the contents. Sadie and Lily watched in fascination as she quickly cleaned and bandaged Eli Turner's head. "Is he alone?" Henry asked.

"Good question," Ma said. "Oscar, best y'have a look 'round."

"Right." He headed for the door, shotgun in hand.

"I'm coming with you," Lily called after him.

"Not unless yer a crack shot, ya ain't. Stay here."

"But what if something happens?" She pressed her lips together in defiance.

He almost laughed, not because she was angry (though she was) or being ridiculous (though, again, she was), but because she looked so adorable. "Nothin's gonna happen, but even if it does, I don't want it happenin' to you—I'd never forgive myself. Now stay here." He went outside.

As he descended the porch stairs, Sadie's question echoed in his mind: what in tarnation was Eli Turner doing way out here? And what had he said about his sister—that someone had Emeline? Were there outlaws in the area? Had she been abducted? Great Scott, what would he do then? If someone had taken the girl, they'd have to go look for her, but Sheriff Hughes would be in charge of that—where was he? Had outlaws struck Clear Creek and abducted her from there? Was Eli part of a posse?

Too many questions, and no answers yet. He hated that.

Oscar checked the perimeter of the house and barn, but nothing was disturbed. Other than the stock wanting to be fed and the cows needing a good milking, things were fine. Nothing seemed to be stirring in the near woods either. He quickly returned to the house to find Eli sitting up, dark hazel eyes blinking, looking utterly disoriented.

"He got quite a bump on his head," Ma said. "Best we take 'im upstairs 'n put 'im in one o' th'guest rooms. He'll rest better there."

"We will in a minute Ma," Oscar said. "Can he talk?"

"'Course I can," Eli snapped. He glanced around the room, still weaving a bit. "Whoa, them varmints got me good."

"What happened?" Oscar asked.

"Some men came through town. They looked familiar—I think they stayed at the hotel in the last month or so, but I cain't remember. I'm not one to go for tea every day, but Emeline did. Maybe they got a look at her and liked what they saw, I ain't sure. Mr. Van Cleet said he watched them leave town, but what brought them back…and…" Eli's eyes rolled up and he crumpled back onto the sofa.

"Now's as a good time as any t'take him upstairs, Oscar," Ma advised.

"All right, Ma," Oscar said. "But when he comes to again, I gotta find out what happened. If there are outlaws 'round here we need to take precautions—and we need to go after Emeline."

"Percautions never hurt nothin', but nobody's

goin' nowhere 'til we find out what's up," Ma said. "'Zat clear, Anson?"

Anson glowered. "Yes, ma'am. But anyone harms even a hair on her head, I'm gonna…"

"Keep yerself in check," Oscar boomed. "Don't let that hot head of yers get in the way."

Lily and Sadie exchanged a look. Neither of them had seen or heard of Anson acting hotheaded before. Apparently they didn't know him as well as they thought.

Oscar carried Eli upstairs to a guest room and laid him on the bed. "Concussion, must be."

Lily entered the room. "What can we do?" she asked.

"None of us can do anythin' 'til he comes to again," Oscar said. "And when he does, Ma always tries to keep someone with this kind of injury awake." He looked at her and at Sadie, who'd just joined them. "That'll be yer job."

They nodded without question.

Oscar put his hands on his hips and glared at the floor. What a day this was turning out to be. And they hadn't even eaten breakfast yet.

Chapter Fifteen

"Then what happened?" Ma asked.

Eli gingerly touched the bump on his head and winced. "If ya ask me, I think they musta overheard somethin' 'bout Oscar's weddin' present from the Cookes…"

"What?" Sadie said in shock. "But they discussed that with Oscar well over a month ago, on his wedding day! How could they…? Wait. You said they looked familiar?"

"I'm sure I've seen them 'round town before, Mrs. Cooke," Eli said.

"Cyrus did have a group of men stay at the hotel about that time," Sadie said. "But would they have waited that long just to get their hands on a measly eight cattle?"

"Beggin' yer pardon, Mrs. Cooke," Eli said. "But 'a measly eight cattle' could mean food for a whole winter for some folks."

"I'm sure it would," Lily agreed. "You'd be surprised what suddenly becomes valuable during hard times. But what I don't understand is what happened to Emeline."

"Well, to tell ya the truth, I ain't sure."

"Wha'd'y'mean yer not sure?" Ma asked. "When'd y'last see 'er?"

Eli repositioned himself on the bed to better look at her. "Emeline kept…now please don't take this wrong, Mrs. White…"

"Go on."

"She kept goin' on 'bout this letter yer son Anson sent, frettin' over it and frettin' over it. Even wrote him back a few times, but she'd always crumple up them letters, throw 'em away and start new ones."

"She did?" Lily said in surprise, glanced at the others and quickly calmed herself.

"You don't think she was on her way here, do you?" Sadie said.

"I hate to say it, but I think so," Eli said.

Sadie began to pace the room. "Now let's not panic until we have this figured out. Logan is supposed to arrive with the cattle today or tomorrow."

"And if them varmints that took my sister are after them, they'd be 'round here too."

"And that's why you're here?" Lily asked.

"Yep. I figger Emeline might've decided to try answerin' Anson's letter in person. Or maybe she just wanted to see what it's like to ride in this direction. I know that sounds silly, but that'd be Emeline. She's kind of a dreamer sometimes."

"You mean she'd saddle a horse and take off for the day, alone, just to…look around?!" Lily asked, aghast.

Eli nodded sagely. "On the surface my sister's one of the most practical gals ya ever did see. But once in a while she gets these notions in her head…"

"So th'men who might be after the Cookes' cattle might've run 'cross her 'n took her with 'em?" Ma asked.

"That's what I think," Eli said. "After all, Emeline's not one to let herself get abducted. In fact, I'd feel sorry for the man fool enough to try."

Sadie nodded. "Yes, that does sound like Emeline." She looked at Ma. "When will Oscar and Anson be back?"

"Any time now," Ma said. "Oscar'll wanna make sure the stock's okay 'n check th'fences, but if those men're after his weddin' present, they'll probably try'n take 'em well 'fore they get here. This place's too busy—too many folks here to stop 'em."

"Stop who?" Anson asked as he came back into the room. "All clear out there, Ma," he added quickly, then turned to Eli. "What are ya talking about? Where's Emeline?"

"Calm down, son," Ma advised. "We've got this figured out. Now we need to decide on what to do next."

"What happened?" Anson asked again in agitation.

"I'll tell him." Lily took Anson by the shoulders and turned him to face her. "It seems Emeline was unable to determine what to do about your letter," she told him calmly. "She was apparently quite emotional—"

Anson's eyebrows shot skyward. "What do you mean?"

"Let me finish. It looks like she may have been riding this way to talk to you, but was waylaid. Perhaps—and this is only our best guess, but perhaps—by a group that found out about the cattle the Cookes are sending here. Some men may have overheard the Cookes talking with Oscar about it and were lying in wait when Emeline stumbled across them. That's the way it looks right now."

Anson took a few seconds to digest that, then turned to Eli. "Ya saw her with these men?"

Eli shook his head, and wished he hadn't. "Mmph. I was trackin' her horse, picked up the trail of a half-dozen riders I figger must've caught up to her, and tracked the lot to 'bout a few hours ride from here. At least I think it was a few hours ride—somebody hit me on the head with somethin', so I don't got a good sense of where I was. Took my horse too. When I came to, I knew I needed help, and this was the closest place, so…" He began to sway.

"We'd best let 'im rest a li'l," Ma said. "Anson, where's Oscar?"

"Checkin' the barn again."

"He'll be back soon, then," his mother said. "'N fer Heaven's sake, where's Henry?"

"Downstairs guardin' the front door," Anson said. "Why?"

Ma rolled her one good eye and shook her head. "Well, least he's doin' his duty—better'n starin' out at th'road. All right, ever'one back downstairs so we can decide what t'do." She laid Eli back down, then shooed everyone else out the door and into the hall.

Lily hung back a moment. "Mr. Turner, er…may I call you Eli?"

"Sure." He settled himself against the pillows.

"Are you hungry?"

"I was 'til I got hit on the head. Now not so much."

"I'll check on you later. You get some rest."

"Mrs. White?"

"Yes?"

"I didn't wanna say this in front of Anson, but… I think Emeline's kinda sweet on him too. But he's so far away, ya know?"

She nodded with a sigh. "Yes, I know. You rest."

"Someone needs to warn Logan," Sadie said.

"Agreed," said Oscar. "I'll go."

"Not this time," Anson said. "I'll do it."

"And get yerself killed?" Oscar countered.

"But I'm the best shot!" Anson argued. "And I know yer worried I'll do somethin' foolish if ya find Emeline, so I'm puttin' myself someplace else."

"Both true. But they're also why ya need to stay here with Henry and protect the family."

Anson was about to retort, but snapped his mouth shut and looked at his mother.

"He's right," his mother said. "I'd feel safer if ya stayed with us."

"Don't worry, Ma," Henry said. "Anson and I'll make sure nothin' happens to ya."

She smiled at her sons. "I know."

"Then it's settled," Oscar said. "I'll find Logan and escort him back here."

"But what about Emeline?" Anson asked. "Who knows what those scoundrels have done to her by now!"

"*If* they have her," Oscar pointed out. "Remember, her brother never actually saw her with them, only that a group of horses had caught up to another horse."

"I don't know," Henry said. "Willie told me Eli Turner's a real good tracker."

Sadie nodded. "He is good—he's tracked quite a few times for Sheriff Hughes before."

Oscar thought a moment. "Well, as I see it, there's only one way to catch these men, provided there are any to catch. That's to lure them out with the Cookes' cattle if that's what they're really after."

"But Emeline!" Anson pleaded.

"And what if they show up here?" Oscar asked. "And poor Henry's left to defend the womenfolk on his own?"

Anson bit his lower lip, probably to keep his mouth shut. It didn't work. "Dagnabit, Oscar! What makes ya think ya can handle six outlaws by yerself?"

Oscar smiled. "Pure size, intimidation and a couple rifles."

"Yeehaw!" Henry whooped. "My brother's gonna pound some heads!"

"Th'only poundin' he needs to do is t'fix th'loose shingles on th'roof," Ma said. "'Member, Oscar, Eli said there were six o'em. There's only one o'ya, two if ya count Logan, 'n I don't like them odds." She turned to Anson. "Son, I know yer sweet on this gal, but we dunno where she is or if these men got 'er. Wisest thing t'do is warn Mr. Kincaid, as he's standin' 'tween them outlaws and the cows. Let's face it, if they want th'cattle bad 'nough, they might kill fer 'em."

"Ma, ya cain't expect me to stand by and let…"

"I can 'spect ya to do as I say, long as yer under my roof, son," Ma said in a voice that allowed no argument. "Now we're gonna get t'Logan first—then ya got yer outlaws. Then ya can ask 'em 'bout Emeline."

Anson stiffened, closed his eyes, but finally nodded in surrender. "Yes, Ma."

Sadie touched his arm. "Your mother's right. You could spend hours or days trying to find these men. Let them come to you, or to Oscar and Logan. They'll have a much better chance of locating Emeline if they're able to interrogate one of them."

"But what are they gonna do to her?" Anson was almost weeping in frustration.

Ma put a hand on his other arm to calm him. "Rest

easy, Anson, we'll tend 'er when we find 'er. She'll be in good hands. And women're valuable in these parts—they ain't gonna kill 'er."

Anson's lip twitched. "If they hurt her… I'll kill them. I'll kill them all."

Ma sighed again. "Anson Ezekiel White, ya'll do no such thing! Last thing that poor girl needs is for ya t'go chargin' in, guns blazin' and puttin' her in worse danger. Now you 'n Henry go out 'n do what needs doin' t'get this place ready fer battle. Oscar'll take care o'yer girl, y'know he will."

Lily and Sadie stood off to one side watching this exchange, mouths flopped open like hooked fish. *Battle?*

Anson, though unhappy, took the hint. He smacked Henry on the arm and nodded at the front door. "C'mon, let's go saddle Oscar's horse."

"I'll get the rifles ready for ya, Oscar," Henry said, then followed Anson out the door.

Oscar went straight to Lily and pulled her into his arms. "Don't worry, Lily Fair. Everything's gonna be all right."

When he released her, she nodded and looked into his eyes. "I know. But please, please be careful."

He gave her a light smile. "Always am." He left the house to fetch his horse and a second rifle.

Lily paced the kitchen.

"Land sakes, chile," Ma said as she put a batch

of cookies in the oven, "stop that 'fore y'wear out th'floor."

"I'm sorry, Ma." She leaned against the dry sink, her hands gripping the edge like a bird's talons. "But this is just like when…"

"When what?" Sadie asked as she poured a bowl of cut-up potatoes into a hot pan. They sizzled and popped in the bacon grease.

"When the soldiers came. The war…"

Sadie looked at Ma, who wrung her hands in sympathy, then back to Lily. "Are you okay?"

Lily relaxed her grip. "Yes. This just brings back a lot of terrible memories."

"I think I understand," Sadie said. "Some of my father's hands went to fight, on both sides. A lot of them never came back."

Lily pressed her lips together and nodded. *Both sides*…for all she knew, some were in Sherman's army that had ravaged and burned…she shook herself. No, she wasn't going to think of such things, not now. She looked at Sadie, saw her sad expression and nodded slowly. "I'm sorry."

"So were we."

"'Nough of this talk, y'two," Ma said. "We got chores t'do, a patient t'take care of 'n a couple hard-workin' men that want breakfast."

Lily and Sadie smiled and got back to work.

Soon breakfast was ready and the five people still in the house (aside from the sleeping Eli) sat at the table. Ma clasped her hands in front of her and bowed her head. "Oh Lord, Ya know what's what wi'this outlaw business, 'n Ya know what's happened to Emeline…"

Lily swore she could feel Anson stiffen in his chair across the table. He sure had it bad for Emeline Turner—she had no doubt he'd take a bullet for her. That made her think of Oscar—would he die to protect her, risk life and limb to keep her safe? Her heart warmed as she realized he was more or less doing that right now.

So what about her—would she do what was necessary if they were threatened? Would she give up her life to save his? She'd seen others do it during the war. She'd done it herself when she tried to save her mother-in-law. How could she do any less for her husband? Why wouldn't she do whatever she could to…

"Amen," Ma concluded.

Lily couldn't suppress her smile. …*to save the man she loved?*

By the time they'd finished breakfast, she was giddy with the realization that yes, *yes*, YES, she was in love with Oscar. And then some. She whipped through the rest of her morning chores in no time, despite the threat of outlaws hanging over them.

"What's going on?" Sadie finally asked as they settled in to do laundry. "You seem awful happy for some reason."

"I am," she said.

"Any particular reason?"

Lily smiled at her. "I love Oscar!"

Sadie laughed. "Well, I'd rather assumed *that*!"

Lily laughed too. "But I wasn't truly sure until today."

Sadie nodded in understanding. "Sometimes we do have to look at it a few times to understand what love is. I didn't fall in love with Harrison right away, but it didn't take me too long to see it was happening. I'd never been in love before—I didn't know what to expect."

"I'd thought I was in love before," Lily mused. "But I think I was really in love with what I could get out of the relationship. My parents and John's were both wealthy plantation owners. We were so smug, so…sure of everything. Then the war began, and he went off to fight, and…" She looked away, her eyes fixed on the barn. "So much has changed since then."

"For the better, I hope," Sadie said.

"Not until recently." Lily shook her head with remembrance. "If you had said that to me a year ago, I would have probably slapped your face."

Sadie put an arm on her shoulder. "I understand. I didn't live through the aftermath of the war, but believe me when I say I understand."

Lily nodded, trusting the woman's words were true. But did it matter? She'd finally found happiness, peace and contentment with Oscar. He'd helped her heal from her scars, was still helping her. She was grateful beyond words.

Sadie gave her shoulder a reassuring squeeze, then bent to their work. "Things will turn out. And who knows, Oscar and Logan might be here in time for supper. We'd better set an extra plate."

"Yes," Lily said. "We'd better." With a smile and just a hint of trepidation, she got to work. *Please, Lord, don't let anyone get hurt. Let them come home safely. Even the cows.*

Chapter Sixteen

"Mr. Kincaid!" Oscar called to the man in the distance. He was still a hundred yards away, but he wanted to alert both Logan and anyone that might be lurking in the brush and trees. If scoundrels were thinking of stealing the cattle, they'd have more than one man to contend with now.

Logan was a few years younger than Oscar but looked a little older, with a handsome, weather-beaten face and brown hair beginning to go gray. He looked up, took off his hat and waved it in greeting. He didn't hurry his charges along, so Oscar kicked his horse into a canter to close the gap. A few of the cattle mooed in protest at the intruder's fast approach, but otherwise stayed together.

Oscar made sure he slowed his horse to a walk when he got closer. "Mr. Kincaid," he said again.

"Oscar, you old scoundrel. I hope you have a batch of those rolls of yours in the oven!"

"Later," he said as he brought his horse alongside Logan's. "I came to escort ya in," he said quietly. "There's been some trouble."

"Trouble?"

"Eli Turner showed up on our doorstep this mornin' after getting' hit on the head. He thinks some outlaws abducted his sister and are comin' after these." Oscar nodded to the cattle.

"What?!"

Oscar scanned their surroundings. "I thought it best we get these home and get some food in yer belly," he said louder.

Logan's eyes darted here and there. "I've seen no one but the normal stagecoaches on this road," he whispered. He knew what Oscar was doing. "That and a rancher or two."

"No trouble, then?"

"None. What's this about Emeline?"

"I ain't sure—what Eli's sayin' don't make much sense. But we figgered if the outlaws got her, better to have them come to us than us runnin' all over the countryside tryin' to find her."

Logan thought a moment. "I can see that. And Eli can't track them if he's got a knot on his noggin. Still…yeah, you're right—something's not making sense. If anyone wanted these beeves, they could've done something about it days ago. There are several spots along this route perfect for an ambush—I'm always extra cautious when I pass through them."

"That's what I was thinkin' on my way to meet

ya," Oscar said. "From the sounds of things, Eli got clobbered 'bout ten miles or so from the stage stop." He looked at the mid-afternoon sun. They wouldn't reach the stage stop until dark—and then only if Logan thought it safe to drive them in by moonlight. Eli must have ridden all night to get clonked on the head and still stagger to the stage stop first thing in the morning… "Ya know, it might've been somewhere right 'round here."

"I see." Logan stilled as he studied the road in front of them, then pulled his Sharps rifle from its scabbard and readied it. "Let's go."

Oscar did the same with his two Winchesters. If there were outlaws waiting for them somewhere, they'd see that the two men were ready for the scoundrels.

The men drove the cattle down the road for hours, undisturbed. "I don't know what Eli was talking about," Logan said. "Like I said before, if there were outlaws after these cattle, they'd have set upon me a long time ago. Unless they're waiting for dark, but stealing them so close to the stage stop?"

"I know, it don't make no sense. But maybe they ain't that smart. I've dealt with dumb outlaws before."

Logan chuckled. "So have I."

"But dumb or not, I don't want them near my wife or family," Oscar added, an edge to his voice.

"I pity the man who gets too close, my friend. I take it you're enjoying married life?"

Oscar looked at him and smiled, but said nothing.

"Yep, nothing like a fine woman to make your life complete," Logan commented with his own smile.

At dusk they reached a small stream that ran parallel to the road for a short distance before meandering off. They watered the animals, let them rest a bit and continued on. If they could just make it to the stage stop unscathed, Oscar could rest easy. But that still didn't explain things.

Anson paced inside the barn, shotgun in hand. He'd seethed over their predicament all day—now that it was well after suppertime, he realized he'd wasted precious energy worrying about something he had no control over. Eli had finally been coaxed into eating something by Lily and was still babbling all sorts of things that made no sense. Ma said he must have gotten hit harder than she first realized. At one point he said he wasn't tracking his sister, just her horse. At another, he couldn't remember tracking anything.

"Give'im a few days, son," Ma had assured. "He'll be hisself again."

"Fine for you to say, Ma," he'd told her. "What happens to Emeline in the meantime?" Had those low-down stinking snakes had their way with her? Was she even still alive? Women were still scarce around here, and men could get desperate for one. After all the things Anson managed to conjure up in his head concerning outlaws and Emeline, he would think she'd have shot herself by now.

"Stop it!" he told himself as he continued to pace. "This is gettin' ya nowhere." Indeed, at this rate he'd be no use to Emeline when they rescued her...if they could find her. The woods were dense and thick for miles around. It would be like finding a needle in a haystack. Ma was right—best use the Cookes' cattle as bait to draw the outlaws out, catch one or two and have them lead Anson, Oscar and Logan to wherever they were keeping Emeline. But the waiting was killing him.

How could he be so sweet on a woman he'd seen only once nearly a year ago? Okay, over the course of one day. Still, he was smitten and had been unable to drive her from his mind ever since. But here he was, armed and ready to spring to her rescue and make any man that dared to harm her pay dearly.

Fueled by Lily's words, he was more determined than ever to make Emeline his. She must have seen something in him too, that fateful day they spied each other on the front porch of the stage stop. Why else would she be "quite emotional," as Lily put it, after receiving his letter? Then again, what if she didn't want to hurt his feelings and didn't know how to tell him she'd just as soon marry a coyote as him?

Anson stopped his pacing and groaned. It could be one as easily as the other. But right now that didn't matter—she was in trouble, and he aimed to rescue her from it. Making sure Emeline was safe and sound no matter what she felt about him was what was important, not to mention reuniting her with her poor brother. Someone would have to look after Eli if his condition didn't improve.

He quickly sent up a prayer to that effect. His heart might be set on Emeline, but he didn't want to have to wonder if he could call on her because she was taking care of a... "No! He's going to be okay, Emeline's going to be okay and I'm..."

An odd sound caught his attention from behind the barn. Maybe he should've lit a lantern—at least he'd be able to see. Then again, you couldn't sneak up on an outlaw without being in the dark. His eyes had adjusted well enough that he could see just fine by moonlight.

Gun at the ready, Anson crept out of the barn to investigate.

"How is he?" Sadie asked quietly as she stepped into Eli's room.

"I think he's better," Lily whispered. She met Sadie halfway between the door and the bed. "Ma said she thinks it's safe to let him sleep now."

"Poor man. I hope he wakes up with all his faculties. All that babble about Emeline... I don't know what to think."

Lily shook her head in dismay. "Neither does Ma. He made sense earlier, but now I don't know what he's talking about."

"You'd think she was sitting home working on

the sewing circle's new quilt the way he talked this afternoon. He's worse than we thought, even if Mrs. White does think it's safe to let him sleep."

Lily raised her hands helplessly. "All we can do is wait and see. I don't know anything about medicine, except what I saw during and after the war."

Sadie studied her a moment. "It was horrible, wasn't it? The war?"

Lily nodded. Sadie wouldn't know firsthand—she came to Oregon before the war, back when it was still a territory, and her father still lived in west Texas. Even when he'd later moved his cattle and household into the territory to be closer to her, both were far from the battles. But she didn't want to talk about those days, especially not once she'd finally been able to move on and start her new life with Oscar. Speaking of Oscar… "I wonder if my husband and your Mr. Kincaid will get in tonight or tomorrow."

"I'm hoping tonight, but mostly I just want them to get here without any trouble. What about Emeline?"

Lily stared at the sleeping form on the bed. "We'll have to wait for Eli to wake up—maybe he'll be able to make better sense of things by then. From the sound of it, I think we're only getting half the story."

"If that."

A shot rang out, making both women yelp with surprise. Only after did they realize they'd jumped into each other's arms. "Goodness, what was that?" Lily asked as she pulled away.

"A shotgun, from the sound of it." Sadie looked at Lily. "Are you all right?"

Lily hugged herself to still her trembling. It had been a long time since she'd heard gunfire, but she was still skittish around it after all these years. Could anyone really forget the ravages of war?

"No return fire," Sadie said. "We'd better find out what happened."

Lily nodded, glanced at a still sleeping Eli and nodded again. Together they went to the door then cautiously made their way down the hall to the staircase. Ma was at the foot of the stairs, a revolver in one hand, the other on her heart. "Ma!" Lily hurried down to her. "Are you all right?"

"Yep, but Henry ran outside."

"Oh no," Lily said. "What if it's the outlaws?"

"Anson's out there. He was checkin' th'barn. Hope they don't stumble o'er each other in th'dark. Henry sometimes gets too excited 'n trips hisself."

"Should one of us check?" Lily asked.

"I'll do it," Sadie said. "I'm no stranger to a gun."

Lily felt a pinch of envy. "You're not?"

"No. You?"

Lily swallowed and started trembling again. "I've held one before. Fired a few times." She closed her eyes against the memory. She'd taken a shot at one of the men setting fire to her home with a pistol, and missed. Badly. She hadn't expected the weapon to have such a kick. After all, she'd seen the men in her family shoot plenty of times and none of them got nearly knocked off their feet.

But she'd had to try and stop those foul men from burning her home. Her poor mother-in-law had already lost her husband, son and plantation to the war and was staying with Lily, hoping against hope that Lily's brother would make it home safe. He didn't. Even if he had, by the time the Union soldiers finished their ugly work, there was no place to come home to…

"Mrs. White, you stay here," Sadie said. "Lily and I will make sure the men are all right."

"Ya sure 'bout this?" Ma asked. "I know I ain't as young's I usta be, but I know how t'use this." She held up the revolver.

"I've no doubt," Sadie said with a smile. She looked at the front door, listening. "Still no return fire. Maybe everything's all right."

"Then why haven't Anson and Henry come back inside?" Lily asked with a sense of dread.

"Maybe Anson's gun went off by accident," Ma suggested. "If so, them boys o' mine're likely out there arguin' 'bout it."

"Yes, perhaps you're right," Sadie agreed. "But we'll be careful anyway. Come on, Lily—let's slip out the back and go around to the barn that way."

"Okay," she said, then looked down at her empty hands. "Um…"

"Here," Ma handed her the revolver. "Take this."

Lily made no comment, just took the weapon.

"Ya know how t'fire one o' these?"

Lily studied it—it wasn't like her father's pistols. She shook her head.

"Watch." Ma took it from her, pulled back the hammer and carefully gave it back. "There. Juss point 'n shoot."

Lily gulped, nodded, then followed Sadie to the kitchen.

They slipped out the back door, made a wide circle to avoid the barnyard and approached the barn from the side. The structure had front and back doors, the front usually open, the back closed. They heard men's voices, more than just Henry's and Anson's and cringed before flattening themselves against the barn's outer wall. "What do we do?" Lily hissed.

Sadie put a finger to her lips to silence her, and Lily felt the heat of embarrassment sting her cheeks. She should know better than to talk, but doggone it, she was a lady. She was the one that was supposed to get rescued, not do the rescuing! She studied Sadie in the moonlight, wondering if she felt just as scared, but it was hard to tell in the dark.

"Lily," Sadie said, barely audible. "Does the barn have windows?"

Lily nodded, held up three fingers, then realized Sadie might not be able to see them. "Three," she whispered back.

Sadie nodded back, then began to slink along the side of the barn to the rear. "What are you doing?" Lily said as quietly as she could.

Sadie motioned her to follow. "I want to see how many men are in there."

They reached the back corner, where there was a knothole in one of the boards. Lily had noticed it a couple of weeks ago and wondered why no one had bothered to cover it. "No need," Oscar had told her. "Too high up for a mouse to get to and too small for a rat. 'Sides, it lets the air in." She felt along the wall, found the hole and peeked through.

A dim light lit the rear of the barn before it faded into shadow. If the men were standing by a lantern, they must be near the front. "I think they're by the barn doors at the front," she told Sadie.

"Okay." Sadie continued on her way.

"What are you doing?!" Lily said in a panicked whisper.

"Maybe it's Oscar," Sadie said.

Lily felt her entire body relax for a second, then tense again. "What if it's not?"

"Only one way to find out," Sadie whispered and slipped around the corner.

Big mistake. Two men stepped out the rear barn door, took one look at Sadie and drew down. Lily, watching from around the corner, jumped to her aid, aiming the revolver at one man and hoping Sadie had hers trained on the other.

One of the men smiled. "Evenin', ladies," he drawled, then eyed the guns in their hands. He looked dirty, disheveled, his clothes unkempt, like he'd been on the trail for a long time.

"Drop your guns," Sadie demanded.

Her nerves twanging, Lily almost dropped hers.

"Not so fast," said the other. "You aren't being smart about this." This man was better dressed, not as dirty, but still looked like he'd been traveling for a while.

"I said, drop them!" Sadie shot back, and Lily gave her a sidelong glance of admiration. The woman had grit.

"And I say we'll shoot your menfolk," the cleaner man said.

Lily felt a sliver of fear go up her spine. So these were the outlaws—and they had Anson and Henry. Her stomach rolled at the thought. "Ohhh," she moaned.

"What'samatter with her?" Dirty asked.

"What do you think?" Sadie spat.

Dirty aimed his gun at Lily, then looked at Sadie. "Drop *yer* guns."

Lily froze. Why couldn't she move? What was wrong with her? She should shoot him! But she didn't, just stared down the barrel of his gun like a scared rabbit.

Sadie narrowed her eyes at him, glowered and let the shotgun fall from her hands.

Chapter Seventeen

"I demand you release us!" Sadie seethed, each word punctuated with fury.

Lily stared at her. So did Anson and Henry, tied back-to-back and shoved into a corner. Gagged as they were, they could offer little explanation for her behavior. Why would she want to provoke the men holding them?

She certainly had the outlaws' attention. After subduing the two women, they'd dragged them into the barn, bound their hands in front of them, hooked Lily's lashed wrists on one of two large spikes protruding from a post (Oscar used them to hang pitchforks on) then forced Sadie to sit on a pile of hay. There were six of them, just as Eli had guessed, and they stood around her in a circle, studying their catch. "Well, is this her?" Clean asked. He seemed to be the leader.

"Yep, purty sure it is," said Dirty. Really, labeling

them thus was the only way Lily could keep track at this point. It was bad enough she had to twist around just to see what was going on.

"If ya ain't sure, then why don't ya just ask?" piped up a third, a straw-haired fellow with pox scars on his cheeks.

His fellow outlaws looked at him, then at each other. Clean rolled his eyes, then glared at Sadie. "What is your name?"

"None of your business!" she spat back.

"Feisty, ain't she?" asked another, one with a drooping mustache.

"Pretty too," said a fifth, even dirtier than Dirty.

"Hands off!" Clean threatened. "If she's the one we want, she is to be kept in one piece."

"What about the other one?" asked Dirty.

Clean looked her up and down. "I don't care what you do with her."

Dirty growled low in his throat. "Makes up for not gettin' to play with the other one."

"We needed a horse, not a hostage," Clean snapped. "Now hush. I'm thinking."

Lily turned away and looked at Anson and Henry, who were both watching the proceedings with interest. After a moment she noticed the two were making tiny movements, subtle enough not to be noticed by their captors. They were trying to loosen or cut their bonds.

Pox Scars walked over to Lily and ran a finger

against her cheek. "This one's sure pretty." He licked his lips. "Can we have her now?"

Lily cringed and shrank away.

"Leave her alone!" Sadie warned.

Clean ignored her words and continued to study her. "Are you Mrs. Cooke of the Triple-C Ranch?"

"What if I am?" she said, eyes narrowed to slits.

"She's kinda scary," Mustache said. "And mean."

"Well?" Clean asked, hands on hips. "Are you or are you not Mrs. Cooke?" He looked at Lily and back, then smiled. "Maybe you need a little encouragement to loosen your tongue." He went to Lily and pulled a knife from a scabbard at his belt.

"I *said* leave her alone!" Sadie yelled, her voice like venom.

"Land sakes, she's mad as a rattler, Jesse!" Pox Scars cried. "I bet she spits poison." So the leader's name was Jesse…

Lily didn't have time to dwell on it, as Jesse grabbed the back of her dress at the collar, almost choking her. "Maybe Mrs. Cooke would like to watch us have a little entertainment." He pulled at Lily's collar, put the knife to her dress and cut through the fabric down to her waist.

She screamed, and the men suddenly went silent. She wasn't sure why for a moment, until the cold night air hit her exposed back…

"Sam Blazes, will ya look at that!" Dirty cried.

"Eeughh!" Dirtier added.

Of course—her back was exposed in all its scarred

glory, eliciting the usual reactions of revulsion from her audience. Good. Lily twisted around just in time to see the outlaws back up as one. "Good Lord, woman, what happened to you?" Jesse asked, eyes wide.

"I don't know about y'all," said Mustache. "But I ain't touchin' that." He shivered and turned away.

Pox Scars shuddered, then fled into a stall. A few seconds later came retching sounds.

"Get away from her!" Sadie yelled.

"Gladly," said the sixth man, a dough-faced youngster, as he backed farther away. "She's like somethin' outta a nightmare."

Lily, her scars serving her well for once, narrowed her eyes, twisted farther around and snarled at them. It was worth a try.

"She ain't human!" Dirtier cried. He wiped his hands over his arms and chest as if brushing off insects.

Lily could only assume that between the lantern light and shadows of the barn, her scars looked worse than normal. That was even better.

"What's the rest of her look like?" Dirty asked as he drew closer. "Leastwise her face is purty."

"It's the same everywhere!" Sadie cried as inspiration struck. "She's got leprosy!"

The outlaws jumped back again, shuddering. "Can we get it?" Dough Face asked with revulsion.

"Yes! So beware!" Sadie said, her voice ominous. "She's in the last stages!"

Lily pulled at her bonds. Her arms were stretched so far over her head she was almost on tiptoe. For lack of a better idea she moaned balefully, then drooled for good measure.

"She's loco, like a rabid coyote!" Dirty cried.

Lily glanced at Anson and Henry, who were vigorously working at their bonds. She had no idea what they were cutting the ropes with, but it seemed to be working. She needed to make sure she kept the bandits' attention. She squinted at Jesse and hissed like a scalded cat.

"Pull yourselves together, you worthless vermin!" Jesse shouted at his men's cries, even as he paled and backed up another step. "You're…you're acting like a bunch of old women! Now get over here—we have a ransom note to write."

"Ohhh, I cain't think straight—cover her up!" Dirty said with a grimace. "That's the most hideous thing I ever did see!"

"Then ya ain't lookin' close enough," came a familiar deep voice near the barn door.

And chaos broke out.

Lily screamed as a gun fired. Dirty flew past her and rolled into Anson and Henry, who had just rid themselves of the ropes and gags. She twisted the other way in time to see Sadie scoot herself forward, lean back, then kick Jesse in the back of the knees to send him sprawling.

Oscar grabbed Pox Scars (just returning from the stall), lifted him up over his head and threw him at

Mustache and Dirtier. Pox Scars' foot hit a lantern that hung from a rope attached to a rafter overhead, the only source of light in the barn. It swung to and fro making eerie shadows of all of them.

Dirty pushed himself up to a sitting position, took one look at Oscar in the flickering light and screamed. Oscar smiled and punched him in the face, swinging underhand. Jesse tried to rise, but Oscar kicked him in the back of the head, landing the ne'er-do-well face first in the hay with a puff of dust. Dough Face collapsed onto his knees, hid his head under his hands and began keening.

Behind Oscar, another man—Logan Kincaid?— began taking the outlaws' guns and tossing them into a nearby stall—thankfully not the one Pox Scars had lost his dinner in. Henry and Anson grabbed Dough Face, yanked him to a standing position and walked him over to Oscar. "Now yer gonna tell us every-thin'!" Anson snarled. "Where's Emeline?"

"Emeline?" Dough Face blubbered. "I don't know no Emeline!"

Anson twisted the man's arm behind his back and yanked upward. *"Where is she?"*

"Anson!" Oscar barked. "Just hold on a minute. Ain't no need to break his arm." He went to Lily, put an arm around her waist and lifted her up, free-ing her wrists from the spike. "Ya all right, honey?"

She smiled, tears in her eyes. "I am now!"

Mustache came to, looked at Oscar and Lily and

yelped in shock. "He's touchin' her! He's got it too! They all got it!"

Oscar turned around and shook his head. "Idiot. They're just burn scars."

Sadie, now on her feet, was letting Logan untie her. "You heard?"

"If you're talking about that whole leprosy thing you came up with, yeah. Well done."

"But why didn't you come in earlier?" Lily asked.

"We were waitin' for Henry and Anson to cut themselves loose," Oscar explained. "We couldn't risk you or Sadie getting hurt by goin' two against six."

Sadie rubbed her wrists. "Thank you, Oscar, Logan. You too, Anson and Henry. The last thing I want to do is get abducted again."

Logan smiled. "I'd imagine."

Oscar set Lily on her feet and began to untie her. "I don't understand," she said to Sadie. "What do you mean 'again'?"

"It's happened before. But I swore to myself years ago I'd never let it happen again. Obviously these men didn't come for the cattle we gifted you—they came for me."

"But what about Emeline?!" Anson gave his prisoner's arm a tug.

"Owwww!" the outlaw wailed. "I told ya, we don't know no Emeline!"

"Yer lyin'! Her brother tracked ya—said she was with ya!"

"Her h-h-horse…"

"Anson, let up," Oscar ordered. He bent over Jesse, who was just coming around, and yanked him to his feet. "Well?"

Jesse blinked at him a few times. "Wha…what?"

"Did ya come here plannin' to make off with Mrs. Cooke?" Oscar gave him a healthy shake.

Jessie grimaced and sighed. "Yes."

"And ya didn't take no other woman along the way?"

"No, just two horses."

"Was one from a woman?" Anson asked.

"Yes, three or four days ago. But we didn't touch her, I swear on my honor."

"On yer honor…" Anson snorted, then exchanged a quick look with Oscar. "Ya mean to tell us ya ran 'cross a woman on yer way here and all ya did was take her horse?"

"Yes! Are you deaf? And last night we did the same with a man. We didn't need *them*. We needed the mounts."

Anson frowned. "Then where's the woman?"

"How should I know!" the outlaw sneered. "She probably walked to some ranch along the road and waited for the next stage to take her home!"

Lily and Sadie gawked at him. "Oh dear," Lily said. "That explains a few things. Including about Eli—he must have been the man they found last night."

"Was Eli that fella?" Dough Face whined. Anson

had let him go, but now Logan had a gun pointed at him. "We just stumbled into him looking for a place to camp. Hezekiah panicked and whacked him on the head."

"Which one's Hezekiah?" Oscar asked.

The outlaws that were conscious pointed at Dirty, who wasn't.

"Ya mean Emeline ain't in danger?" Anson asked in disbelief.

"Would ya rather she was, little brother?" Oscar asked. "Sounds to me like Eli followed her horse's tracks until she met with this bunch, missed her footprints somehow and stayed on her horse's trail until he got himself clobbered. Sound about right?" A couple of the outlaws nodded. "Shoot, Emeline's prob'ly home safe and sound, wonderin' where her brother's gotten off to."

"What I don't understand," Lily said, "is why Eli didn't get help."

Sadie smiled. "Isn't it obvious? He didn't want folks to know his sister ran off after some man. Even in Clear Creek, that would get tongues wagging. She wasn't thinking of such things, of course—knowing Emeline, she just thought she was off on a romantic adventure. It's the sort of thing headstrong girls her age are prone to do."

Lily nodded in understanding. "I can see that."

Jesse grimaced and coughed. "Disgusting."

Sadie turned to him. "Since when is love disgusting?"

That got Anson's attention. "Love?"

"What woman in her right mind would want to live in a place like this?" Jesse spat. He looked around, his eyes settling on Oscar, Henry and Anson. "Or be married to the likes of you?"

"I would," Lily said, her voice stern. "These men are my family and I love them."

He laughed in scorn. "Big talk for an abomination."

Oscar pulled his arm back. "That's my wife yer addressin', mister!" He got in his face. "The most beautiful woman in the world, I'll have ya know. And I love her!" One punch, and Jesse fell to the ground with a thud, unconscious.

Lily's eyes lit up. "Oscar! You do?"

"'Course I do, Lily Fair. Cain't ya tell?"

She smiled. "I think I've known all along. I've just never heard you say it."

He took her in his arms. "I guess I'd rather show ya, Lily Fair." He kissed her tenderly on the mouth, then gazed into her eyes. "Ya ain't said it neither, but I know ya love me."

"Y-you do?"

He nodded. "I can see it in yer eyes, the way ya walk now, yer voice. Before, you were all fearful—'fraid of who'd see ya, judge ya by them scars." With his fingers, he traced the marks on her back, caressing them. Loving the pain away.

Lily wanted to bury her face in his chest. He was

right, of course—he'd freed her from all of that. She returned his look. "I love you."

A low whimper broke the spell. Everyone looked to see a now-conscious Pox Scars staring at Oscar and Lily, tears in his eyes. "Well, goldang, if that ain't the most beautiful thing I ever did hear, I don't know what is." He sniffled.

Henry looked at the outlaw, then at Oscar and Lily, and burst out laughing. "He done called it, Oscar—ya love Lily no matter what!" He looked at Pox Scars again. "Bet ya never seen nothin' like that before, have ya?"

Pox Scars shook his head. "Nossir, I sure haven't. I…well, I hope someday a woman can love me like that, even though I…" He sighed and rubbed his own scars.

Henry laughed again. "Oscar, you done poked a hole in his evil ol' heart!"

Everyone looked again at the pockmarked outlaw, who but moments ago had rape and who knows what else on his mind. A miracle, when it came down to it.

Oscar turned back to Lily. "See, Lily Fair? The Lord uses all things for good, even yer scars. Ya just had to learn to let Him. For me, that makes ya the prettiest gal around." He kissed her again.

As his words sank in, Lily began to understand the meaning of the term "beauty from ashes." The ashes had left her wounded and afraid—until Oscar saw the beauty in her.

Epilogue

Three weeks later...

"Then it's all arranged," Harrison Cooke said happily. "Don't worry, Mrs. White, we'll take good care of your boy. Though he's hardly a boy anymore."

Ma smiled at Anson. "No, he sure ain't. I'd like him t'stay, but ya gotta let a man get a chance at happiness. Ya cain't very well court a gal through the mail t'see if th'two o' ya will suit." She opened her arms to her son, tears in her eyes.

Anson stepped into them. "Thanks, Ma. I'll never forget this."

"'Course ya won't—I ain't gonna let ya! But if it don't work out, ya juss c'mon back."

Anson hugged his mother tight. "I know. But if Emeline's fool enough to ride this way for a whole day and get her horse stolen, well, she's gotta feel somethin' for me, right?"

Harrison laughed. "Right now she's still too embarrassed about losing her mare to those outlaws to set her cap for anyone. But at least she got her back, thanks to you and your brothers."

"Yeah," Anson agreed. "They sure were a dumb bunch of outlaws."

"That 'dumb bunch' almost got hold of my wife," Harrison reminded him. "You kept her from being abducted—I can't thank you enough for that. The least I can do is give you a position at the Triple-C for a time so you can court Emeline."

"Does she know Anson's comin'?" Oscar asked as he emerged from the kitchen carrying a pan of hot rolls.

"She don't," Ma assured him. "We ain't even tole Willie yet. But he'll bring us Anson's letters, so we know what's up."

Lily entered the room with a tureen of stew and set it next to the rolls. Harrison had arrived two hours before, informed them of his plan to help Anson and Emeline, and inspected the animals he'd given them while the family considered it. He was tired and hungry, so she and Oscar had heated up some stew from the night before and made a fresh batch of rolls. She smiled at Harrison, then went to Oscar and hugged him.

He hugged her back, kissed the top of her head, then turned to Anson. "Ya do understand what love is, don't ya, little brother?"

Anson blushed. "'Course I do. Ain't nothin' to

it—ya get to feelin' all funny inside, like your belly's full of butterflies. Ya cain't eat, cain't sleep, cain't think straight…"

"Oh Lawd," Ma said, rolling her eyes.

"Young man, that's only the start," Harrison replied, looking at the rolls. "There's a lot more to love than a few butterflies in your stomach."

"Love is accepting a person for who they are," Lily added. She looked up at Oscar and smiled. "Knowing the other person's weaknesses and shortcomings, and loving them anyway, unconditionally."

He smiled back. "Through sickness and health, 'til death do us part."

"And then some," she added. "Up to and including a band of idiot outlaws."

Oscar laughed and kissed her on the nose. She snuggled closer and leaned her head against his shoulder, and he tightened his arm around her in response. "It also means being willin' to take a bullet for the one ya love, come to that," he said. "Those outlaws might've been dumb, but as ya recall some guns went off. It was darn lucky none of us got shot."

Anson looked at Harrison. "Yer sure Sadie's doin' all right?"

Harrison laughed. "My wife is made of tougher stuff than you can imagine. Thank Heaven you, Oscar and Henry saved the day or I'd have to listen to her complain of her ordeal for months. She abhors abduction."

"Ain't nobody like't, I figger," Ma said, then looked around. "Where's Henry?"

"Out on the front porch," Oscar said. "Where else?"

"Again?"

"What's so unusual about him being on the front porch?" Harrison asked.

"He's waitin' for the stage," Oscar explained. "A schoolmarm named Norton passed through here some weeks ago, headin' to The Dalles. Henry was smit. He's wantin' her to come back."

"Oh, the poor chap," Harrison said.

Just then, they heard the stage pulling in. Everyone turned to the front door. "Hmmm, few minutes early," Ma said. "Oscar, best y'feed Mr. Cooke in th'kitchen or those passengers're gonna devour th'rolls ya made fer 'im."

"Right, Ma." Oscar let go of Lily, picked up the stew pot in one arm and the pan of rolls with his free hand. "Follow me, Mr. Cooke. And thanks again for comin' all the way out here to offer Anson a job on the Triple-C—mighty kind of ya."

"Think nothing of it. Besides, I wanted some of those delicious rolls. And to see how the cattle were faring. All in all, I'd say they're…"

"He did it!" An excited Henry burst in from the porch. "He did it, Ma, He did it!"

Ma blinked in confusion. "Who'd what?"

"The Lord, Ma! I prayed He'd bring her back and He did!" Henry spun on his boot heel and rushed back outside.

Everyone's jaw went slack. Harrison cocked his head to the side as he heard Henry's voice, then a woman's. "Was he referring to…?"

"I believe he is." Oscar glanced up a moment, as if double-checking with the Almighty, then looked at the door just as Henry opened it, escorting a tired but happy Evangeline Norton into the front room. The little group's eyes widened at the sight of her on Henry's arm. From the look of it, she was the only passenger.

"Thank you so much, Mr. White," Miss Norton told Henry as he led her straight to the table. "I'm quite famished."

Oscar shrugged and set the food back down. Harrison, concern on his face, quickly sat as Henry pulled a chair out for the woman.

"I'm so angry, I can't tell you," she went on. "Oh, but I mustn't complain about my problems to you. I'm so sorry."

Henry sat next to her. "I don't mind. 'Sides, maybe I can help."

Harrison, recognizing his chance might disappear, took two rolls and hid them under his napkin while everyone's attention was elsewhere.

"But…you can't, you see…" She pulled a lace handkerchief from her reticule. "No one can. I don't know what to do." She blew her nose as the first tears fell.

Henry looked at his mother. "She got cheated outta her job, Ma. The town done hired a man and let

him have her position. She told me so on the porch."
Like Oscar, he looked up, but with a wide, knowing smile as Miss Norton blew her nose again.

Ma glanced between the two, sighed, then looked at Anson. "Yer goin' t'work fer Mr. Cooke's gonna leave a right big hole to fill. Gonna be lotsa extra work 'round here."

Henry's face lit up. So did Oscar's. "Ma?"

She nodded to herself. "Yep. Might need t'hire someone. But findin' a body right away'll be tricky."

Henry began to chuckle, while Oscar put his hand over his face. "Ma..."

"Don't matter if't's a man or a woman..."

"Ma!"

"So do ya want the job?" Henry blurted at Miss Norton.

She wiped her eyes with the handkerchief and stared at him. "Wha...what job?"

"Bringin' in wood, cleanin' out stalls, scrubbin' floors, helpin' in th'kitchen," Ma said. "Maybe keepin' Henry's fingers outta the cake frostin'. Ain't purty work, but't's work."

"Job?" Miss Norton repeated, still not catching on.

"And ya can go fishin' with me and help catch dinner sometimes," Henry said excitedly.

Miss Norton looked around the room as Harrison snuck a third roll. "Are you saying you're offering me a job?" she asked, stunned.

"Take it!" Henry urged. "Then ya won't have to worry none about nothin'!"

Miss Norton, a hand to her chest, slowly smiled. "You're offering me work?"

"Pay ain't much," Ma continued. "But ya'd have yer own room, though ya might hafta share it on 'ccasion with a passenger. 'N three meals a day." She looked at Oscar. "Sound 'bout right?"

Oscar's brow furrowed. He opened his mouth to speak, saw the look on Henry's face, and let himself smile. "Yeah, sounds 'bout right, Ma." He put an arm around Lily again and shrugged.

Lily laughed and looked at Miss Norton. "We'd love to have you stay. I'm sure you'd enjoy working here—you can try it for a while and see if you like it. After all, what have you got to lose?"

Miss Norton quickly put a hand over her mouth to stifle a sob. "Thank you, thank you so much. I prayed for a miracle to happen ever since I found out my position had been given away, and…" She couldn't talk, just wept.

Henry smiled proudly and looked at everyone in turn. "Yeah, the good Lord knows what He's doin'. He puts folks right where they need to be if they let Him."

Oscar and Lily exchanged another look. "That He does," Oscar said.

"Yes, He certainly does," she replied.

"Amen to that," Harrison said, and, unable to wait any longer, he took a generous bite of one of Oscar's famous rolls.

* * * * *

"You don't ever complain. You take care of someone else's *kinder* without hesitation, and you're giving them a home they haven't had in who knows how long."

"Trust me. There was plenty of hesitation on my part."

"I do trust you."

Beth Ann's breath caught at the undercurrent of emotion in his simple answer. "I'm glad to hear that. I got a message from their social worker this afternoon. She was supposed to come tomorrow, which is why I stayed home today to make sure everything was as perfect as possible before her visit."

"I wondered why you didn't come to the project house today."

"That's why, but now her visit is going to be the day after tomorrow. What if she decides to take the children and place them in other homes? What if they can't be together?"

Robert paused and faced her. "Why are you looking for trouble? God brought you to the *kinder*. He knows what lies before them and before you. Trust *Him*."

"I try to." She gave him a wry grin. "It's just…just…"

"They've become important to you?"

She nodded, not trusting her voice to speak. The idea of the three youngsters being separated in the foster care system frightened her, because she wasn't sure what they might do to get back together.

"Don't forget," Robert murmured, "as important as they are to you, they're even more important to God." His smile returned. "How about getting some Christmas pie before we have to fish three *kinder* out of the brook?"

With a yelp, she rushed forward to keep Crystal from hoisting Tommy to see over the rail. Robert was right. She needed to enjoy the children while she could.

Don't miss
An Amish Holiday Family *by Jo Ann Brown,*
available November 2020 wherever
Love Inspired books and ebooks are sold.

LoveInspired.com

LIEXP1020

Love Harlequin romance?

DISCOVER.

Be the first to find out about promotions,
news and exclusive content!

f Facebook.com/HarlequinBooks

𝕏 Twitter.com/HarlequinBooks

⊙ Instagram.com/HarlequinBooks

P Pinterest.com/HarlequinBooks

ReaderService.com

EXPLORE.

Sign up for the Harlequin e-newsletter and
download a free book from any series at
TryHarlequin.com

CONNECT.

Join our Harlequin community to
share your thoughts and connect
with other romance readers!
Facebook.com/groups/HarlequinConnection

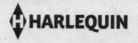